The Three Heads
of
Cerberus

by
Alan Gibbons

First published in Great Britain in 2012
by Caboodle Books Ltd
Copyright © Alan Gibbons 2012

A Catalogue record for this book is available
from the British Library.

ISBN 978 0 9569 482 81

Cover design by Andrew Minchin
Page Layout by Highlight Type Bureau Ltd
Printed by Cox and Wyman

The paper and board used in the paperback by
Caboodle Books Ltd are natural recyclable products
made from wood grown in sustainable forests.
The manufacturing processes conform to the environmental
regulations of the country of origin.

Caboodle Books Ltd
Riversdale, 8 Rivock Avenue, Steeton, BD20 6SA
www.authorsabroad.com

Story one: the first head of Cerberus

One

I race across the ground. The stones slide and crunch underfoot. My heart is thudding. My eyes dart left. They dart right. The world shifts and pitches around me as I weave through the crowd. My breath comes in short bursts. My blood is pumping. He's here somewhere, the assassin, the killer. I shoulder the ZX90 assault rifle. It is feather light, not like a weapon at all, more an extra limb, but deadly nonetheless. The computerised night sight appears in my contact lenses. Where the hell is he? Where's Xavier? There are figures in the grainy emerald haze. One of them is him, Arden Xavier, mercenary, contract killer, No 1 threat to the peace of the galaxy. But which one is he? How do you spot one bug-human hybrid among so many? How do I tell a hired gun from the diplomat he has come to kill? They all belong to the same gene pool.

I swallow hard. If I get this wrong an innocent man dies. That man dies and we have inter-galactic war. Planets are reduced to ash. Whole populations perish. Some mission when the President and his would-be assassin are all but identical down to the pincers on the end of their shiny, little arms. It's a dirty war. It is hard to tell friend from foe. Sweat starts from my palms.

I have to make a split-second decision. The responsibility makes my head spin. I run what I know about Xavier through my mind. He is three metres tall. He has the dome-shaped head common to all life forms from the Threnassic planetary system. Though he usually stands erect on two legs like a human, he has three more pairs of limbs that he employs to deadly effect. All three pairs end in lethal pincers. None of this helps. I am moving through a crowd of Threnassics. They all have similar domed bug heads. They all have multiple pairs of legs. All but one is vital to the peace effort. They are politicians, diplomats, ambassadors. Most vital of all is President Krenatki Shavlotan, the

Threnassic Peace Laureate. He is the best damned bug-man this side of the Milky Way. Today he starts his second term as President of Thren 15 with a peace conference. He is the only politician who can prevent a slide to war. The conflict could cost millions of lives.

"Henry."

I try to blot my mother's shout from my mind. I weave through the crowd, trying to focus on each face in the eerie, greenish murk. One of them is Xavier, but which one?

"Henry!"

I twist the barrel of the ZX90. I didn't want to use the Night Bloom feature, but I've got no choice. If I don't act I'm going to lose him in the crowd. The Night Bloom banishes the sweating darkness. Suddenly the area around me is as bright as a summer's day. A face lurches into view. Not him. Another face. No, not that one either. Then there he is, Arden Xavier, fleeing through the crowd. I notice his one distinguishing feature, the melted stub of an antenna, the result of a shoot-out with Shavlotan's bodyguards the last time he tried to assassinate the great man.

"Can you hear me, Henry?"

I try to focus. My finger teases the trigger. I tense, relax, tense again. I've only got one shot at this, one shot to save the galaxy from possible annihilation.

"Henry Kwok! You answer me this instant!"

I curse under my breath and tug the control gloves from my hands. Boiling with frustration, I throw them onto my bed. Thanks a bundle, Mum. I shake my head. One day she is going to give me a break, but I'm not holding my breath. My mum is to hands off parenting what Genghis Khan was to world peace.

"Coming, Mum."

I stamp downstairs. How does she do it? Every time I get to a vital stage of the game she calls me to the dinner table or tells me I've got homework to finish or reminds me that I promised to take care of my pain in the neck sister Anna.

4

"What is it?" I snap as I stamp into the living room.

"Don't take that tone with me, young man," she says, frowning.

OK, I tell myself, time to make with the apologies and grovel. I've got something to ask her. No way is she going to say yes if I rub her up the wrong way.

"I need you to do me a favour," she says.

She needs *me* to do *her* a favour? How cool is that?

"I've got a special delivery coming between noon and 1pm tomorrow, but I've a business appointment and your dad is out of town."

"Where is he this time?"

"New York."

Oh yes, I took a call from him last night. He said he was in some swanky Manhattan hotel. He described the room, showing off, talking about what was in the mini bar and how many channels there were on the TV. The view was to die for. Glittering skyscrapers, five-star restaurants. You know the deal.

"We might be moving there."

"The Big Apple?"

"Yes, we're going to be pips."

Funny, Mum. Not!

"So I need you to be in," she concludes.

"Sure."

She smiles for the first time.

"How long are you going to be gone?" I ask.

"I'll be home about seven in the evening," she answers.

Even cooler. That makes the next question easier. I can make up a story instead of telling her the truth.

"Can I go to James's once I've collected the parcel?"

That's James Wong, my best friend. His dad is from San Francisco. His mum is London Chinese. He's new to school, but it's as if he's been around forever.

"He lives right across the city," she says doubtfully.

I'm ready with an answer.

"His mum will pick me up."

"You can't go until my parcel comes," she says. "It's the pull-up stands for my presentation. It's really urgent."

"Don't worry," I tell her. "I'll be in."

She pats my cheek.

"You're a good boy, Henry."

I'm hardly a boy. I'm fourteen. I decide not to say anything. It's this thing, the thing I have to do, the most important thing ever. I visualise my destination, a computer game store next to the Noodles Shop on Wan Chai Road. I know the area. It's near the Nam Hoy building. That's where I'm going to meet him, the man who changed my life.

"Maybe," she says, turning the request over in her mind.

"Please, Mum. You know James. Plus you've met his mum."

"Have I?"

She hasn't, but I know I can persuade her that she has. I've done it before. I just have to choose moments when her mind is on other things, like today. She's all excited about the presentation she's doing tomorrow. She listens kind of absent-mindedly while I make up Mrs Wong's life story, the family in London, the First at Oxford, the job that brought her back to her Hong Kong roots. Why do I have to make it up? Simple. I don't know anything about James's mum. James has only been around for a term and I don't know much about his parents. His mum could be half Wookie, half cookie for all I know. He's probably told me about his family, but it never seemed important enough to listen.

Until now.

"OK, but you have to wait in until my delivery comes. Promise."

"I already did!"

"So promise again. It's important. I know you, Henry. If you get distracted by that game, nothing else can get your attention."

"I promise. May all the horrors of Hell break loose over my innocent head if I let you down."

6

She smiles.

"You're a good kid, Henry."

I nod. That's me. Henry Kwok. The good kid. Works hard. Gives his assignments in on time. Straight As in all subjects. Never been in trouble at school. Not ever.

I'd love to do something really wild, but I know I never will. I'm the good kid. That makes the meeting on Wan Chai Road even more important. My mind snaps back to the day I got hooked on the game.

The Three Heads of Cerberus.

I was posting rubbish on Facebook when I got this weird pop-up. It was the monster of myth, Cerberus, the three-headed hound that guards the gates of the Underworld. I clicked on impulse and I found myself on the start-up menu of a game. It had me hooked right away. I got to the end of the first level and it asked me to fill out an online form. My parents have always said I shouldn't give out any details to people on the Net. They're always going on about online safety, but man, this was addictive. It was the best game ever. You hear people say they've played some realistic games, but there's never been a game like this. It's as if the room dissolves around you. Reality melts away and all that's left is your computer game character fighting for his life in an alien world. Maybe that's what Mum is getting at.

"Henry?"

I turn to look at her.

"Did you say something?"

She purses her lips.

"I've been saying something for the last couple of minutes. Don't you ever listen to me? You don't pay attention when your head is full of those games."

Not *those* games.

The game.

She goes on about her delivery...again! I tell her she's got no reason to worry. I'll be in. Finally, she seems satisfied. I sit in front of the TV, but

I'm not watching it. I'm remembering the email. I played Level One on the Monday. The email came on the Tuesday. This is what it said:

Impressed with our game, The Three Heads of Cerberus? If you are, why don't you join the Cerberus Trialling Group? We value your input in designing the digital entertainment systems of the future.

So what's in it for you? Group members will receive each level of the game as it is developed. You get an exclusive preview of every thrilling moment. As if that isn't exciting enough you will be able to give the game's designers feedback. Just think, your ideas might find their way into the best interactive entertainment package ever!

I wanted to be involved. Of course I did. But meet a stranger at a store on Wan Chai Road? That sounded scary. All that stuff about staying safe online, I was about to break a cardinal rule. But I was going to do it. All my life I'd been the good boy. Now I was going to take a risk.

The first one ever.

It was a wild thing to do, completely out of character. But it was exciting too. Yes, I was going to be a bad boy for a day. I stared at the email for ages. There was a tick box. All I had to do was click once agreeing to join the Cerberus Trialling Group and I would receive details. Three times I went to click. Three times I pulled my hand away. The fourth time I clicked. That's how I got the address on Wan Chai Road.

And a name.

Schlachthof. Liesl Schlachthof.

I knew what it meant, of course. I'm not stupid.

Schlachthof.

Slaughterhouse.

Cool name...if you're a grade A psycho.

Every time I read the name of the woman I am going to meet, alarm bells ring. But I'm going through with it. I have to. OK, I know all the warnings about Internet safety off by heart, but the game is so cool I can't say no. So there is just one thing I've got to do and that's set the time for my appointment. I eat with Mum and Anna. We talk about school and the holiday we're going to take when Dad gets back from his business trip. I say Australia. Anna says Kuala Lumpur. Mum says we will have to compromise. That probably means we're going to KL. Somehow Anna always gets her way.

As soon as I've done enough of the family stuff I make my way upstairs. The game is still running, waiting for me. That's the way I've always thought about the game, as if it's a living thing, a human intelligence. It isn't just that it's real. It's *personalised*. It seems to know what makes me tick. It's programmed with the thoughts, hopes and dreams of me, Henry Kwok. Somehow, it anticipates me. It knows all my interests, all my instincts. That makes it scary. It also makes it compulsive. I touch the mouse to activate it. I snap on the control gloves. It starts the way it always does, with a quiz. A question appears. I've got to type the answer in thirty seconds or the game locks me out for twenty-four hours.

Q. What is a wormhole?

A. A wormhole is a scientific hypothesis. It is a 'shortcut' through spacetime.

Q. How does it work?

A. Consider spacetime visualised as a two-dimensional (2D) surface. If you fold along a third dimension you can make a wormhole 'bridge'. Theoretically, you can make a tunnel with two ends each in separate points in spacetime.

Q. Who are the most famous theoreticians of the wormhole?

A. John Archibald Wheeler and Hermann Weyl.

Q. Why do wormholes matter?

A. If they exist things like time travel and inter-universal travel become possible.

The game is satisfied. The question screen dissolves. I'm back in the crowd of Threnassics chasing Arden Xavier, terrorist, assassin, master criminal. I glimpse him vanishing around a corner. I barge my way through the startled aliens shouting his name.

"Xavier," I yell. "Arden Xavier!"

I turn the corner and hear the telltale hum of Xavier's weapon. The power flash bites a chunk out of the wall next to me. I drop to one knee, feeling the rush of heat across my scalp then I return fire. The ZX90 blows out the window to Xavier's left. He stares at the damage and grins. "Poor shot, Kwok," he chuckles.

I freeze. Kwok. Did he just say Kwok? The game has changed. Up to this moment I've been a character in the game. I've been known simply as M. Suddenly M has ceased to exist. Instead I am myself. I am Henry Kwok, intergalactic agent. That form I filled in, the game has used my details to develop a character and the character is me.

Cool.

I mean coolissimo.

Then I see something that makes me snap out of it. I push the shock of hearing my name to the back of my mind. Xavier has me in his sights. I pitch forward as he fires and execute a forward roll. Before I can get to my feet the power flash hits me. It isn't a direct hit. I'd be dead if it was. But it smacks me in the face like an invisible hand. The aftershock swats me against the wall knocking the air from my lungs. Xavier drops onto three pairs of his legs, scuttling towards me like a giant beetle. He's going to fire again. I have to respond. Got to. Got to...

But he fires, hits me in the chest. I'm dead. I tear off the control gloves and shout my frustration. I hear Mum's voice float up the stairs.

"Are you OK, Henry?"

"Yes, Mum," I answer. "I'm fine."

"That computer game again?"

"Yes, Mum," I tell her. "Just the computer game. I got killed again."

Just the computer game. Who am I kidding? This isn't just entertainment. It is way more important than that. I know what's coming. My controller is going to speak to me, tell me where I've gone wrong. The controller is a shadowy face and a scrambled, robotic voice. Only it isn't, not this time. I'm in for my second surprise of the evening. I find myself staring at a stunning blonde, twenty-four, twenty-five years old. She's got these electrifying, sky-blue eyes. I mean wow.

Just wow.

"My name is Schlachthof," she says, "Liesl Schlachthof. I am your controller."

"But you're the woman I'm going to meet. You're waiting for me at the games store on Wan Chai Road."

"That's right," she says.

I stare in disbelief. This isn't a prepared script. She's talking to me.

"Can you see me?" I ask. "You know, see me, hear me, like some sort of video phone?"

"That's right," Schlachthof replies.

"What kind of game is this?" I ask.

"A very good one," she says. "You must have worked it out by now. The Three Heads of Cerberus is a new type of game, a game like no other. It is a whole new world and the screen is its portal."

I can't think of a thing to say so Schlachthof carries on talking.

"You know your problem?" she asks.

"No."

"You're easily distracted. You let your mother distract you earlier."

"My mother's good at distracting people," I say ruefully, but Schlachthof isn't listening.

"Then you lost focus again when you heard your name. You've got to do better than that."

"I will," I promise.

"I know you will," she says. "You get better or you get dead."

I utter a protest.

"It's only a computer game."

The moment the words are out of my mouth I regret them. I've just betrayed the game. Schlachthof's dazzling eyes narrow.

"You don't believe that."

"No," I confess. "I don't."

"So listen to me and listen good," she says. "You get better or you get dead. End of."

"I'll get better," I tell her.

"Because?"

"Because I don't want to get dead."

"And?"

Now what does she want from me?

"And?"

My mind races. Then I've got it.

"Because my mission has to succeed. I have to protect the President and preserve the peace of the galaxy."

"Got it in one. See you tomorrow, Henry."

"Yes, see you tomorrow, Schlachthof."

She smiles.

"Call me Liesl."

With that she's gone. I shut down the game. See you tomorrow, Liesl Schlachthof.

TWO

I'm in luck. The delivery comes at noon. It gives me all the time I need. Half an hour later I'm turning right out of Wan Chai Metro and weaving between the lunchtime traffic. There's the Noodles Shop and, next to it, kind of grubby and tired, the games store. I mentioned it to the biggest computer game geeks in our class, but none of them knew anything about it. As I open the door and stare at the dingy interior I wonder how such tacky, unimpressive premises could be associated with a game as impressive as the Three Heads of Cerberus. As I am about to find out, appearances can be deceptive. The bell above the door tinkles. Old-fashioned or what? For a few moments I stand in the middle of the room, waiting for somebody to come. Then there she is, Liesl Schlachthof. She was gorgeous on the screen. Double that in real life. Plus some.

"You're early," she says.

"Mum's package came on time," I reply.

She smiles. "Come this way."

I follow her up the stairs. I try not to look, but it's hard not to fix my stare on the sway of her hips.

"Are you looking at my butt?" she asks.

Of course I am looking at her butt. What am I, dead?

"No," I croak. "Honest."

That just makes her laugh. She leads the way into an upstairs room. I stop dead. The contrast between this gleaming, ultra-modern space and the shabby room downstairs couldn't be more dramatic. It's windowless, but bright and airy somehow. I try to work out how it's done and come up clueless.

"Why don't you make downstairs look like this?" I ask.

"Because, Henry," Liesl answers, "I don't want anyone knowing what we've got up here. I've made the shop frontage as unappealing as possible."

"Oh."

I examine my surroundings. There's a row of computer screens.

"Cool machines," I observe.

I'm impressed. They are wafer thin and seem to hover in the air. I strain to see how they are held in place.

"Where's the keyboard?" I ask, looking closer.

"There isn't one. Let me show you. Stand here."

She indicates a spot in front of the computer. I shuffle into position.

"Now imagine the keyboard and start typing."

"What?"

"Can you touch type?"

"Yes, my mum taught me."

"So you know the way around a QWERTY keyboard. Try to picture it and type the way you would on a conventional keyboard."

I feel stupid, but soon I'm air-typing. To my astonishment, the letters and words appear. There are a few mistakes, but I'm getting the hang of it.

"I don't believe it!"

"Why not? It's just an extension of the technologies being developed in your time."

"My time? You mean....?"

"That's right," Liesl says. "I'm from the future."

I wait a beat then laugh. "No. No way. You're making fun of me."

Liesl looks disappointed in me.

"Don't act stupid, Henry. It doesn't suit you. Are you really trying to tell me you didn't suspect something like this?"

What am I meant to say? Either way, I end up sounding pathetic.

"I knew the game was very advanced."

"When you were chasing Xavier, where did you think you were?"

I relive the experience of racing through the crowd of Threnassics. I could feel the metallic floor beneath my feet, smell the chemical mist that hung in the air, feel the brush of bug tentacles.

"Thren 15, hub of the Threnassic transportation network."

"And you were right? Cerberus isn't a game. It's a training module."

I frown. "What have you been training me for?"

"Your mission, of course."

I stare at her for a few moments and that's a pretty easy thing to do then I pull a face.

"No," I tell her, "this is all too far-fetched."

"If you don't want to be involved," she says, her glance drifting away, "you know where the door is."

Her tone surprises me. She's gone from friendly to icy in a matter of seconds. Her blue eyes fix mine a second time. There is the ghost of a question in her stare.

"You're still here," she says, kind of superior, kind of relieved.

"I've got to know about Cerberus," I mumble.

"No more silly questions?" she asks. "No more pretending to be more stupid than you are?"

"No."

"No wasting your natural gifts?"

I've got natural gifts? Hey, she just said something nice about me.

"No, I'll do anything you say."

"Good. Then we can do business."

"What kind of business?"

"Saving the universe, of course."

I am tempted to object, ask her if she's kidding, but I resist it. The last thing I want is another of those frosty, disappointed stares.

"What's my part in this?"

Liesl takes a deep breath, a sure sign that she is embarking on a long story.

"Why do you think you're here, Henry?"

I answer honestly. "I've no idea."

"I think you do."

I stare for a moment.

"I've been chosen."

"That's right. You've been chosen. What have you been chosen for?"

"A mission."

"Right again. What is your mission?"

She's got me stumped. What am I supposed to say? I go back to the game. My mind is racing. All I can think of is the bug-man Arden Xavier. "I have to find Arden Xavier. I have to stop him assassinating the President and destroying the peace of the universe."

I wait. A clock ticks. My cheeks burn. I feel so stupid.

"Spot on," Liesl says after the longest time.

"That's your mission. Your training's gone well so far." She pulls out a Smartphone. "92%. That's very impressive, Henry. You're nearly ready. What score do you have to reach before we can use you?"

"100%?"

"I like your style. 99% will do."

Big of her!

"And if I fall below it?"

"I'm sorry. Failure is non-negotiable. You will achieve 99%. You get the score or you get..."

"Dead?"

"Right."

"How long have I got?"

"A week."

It sounds like a tall order. I know I'm close, but it's getting harder. She passes her hand over a glowing panel and a panorama forms.

"Recognise it, Henry?"

"It's the Peak."

"That's right. What do you see?"

"Victoria Harbour. Kowloon."

"Anything else?"

I'm not sure what she wants. She just loves making me feel inferior.

"People, Henry. What you see is a thriving city of seven million people. How many people in the world, Henry?"

I know this one.

"Seven billion. Give or take the odd sister who might be an alien."

She ignores me.

"And a century from now?"

I shrug. "I don't know."

"Fifteen billion. A few decades later, what do you think?"

"Twenty billion?"

"Pretty close. The planet's resources are exhausted. Life is becoming impossible so we take to the star ways. Millions take flight on huge transporters and set off in search of planets that can sustain life. Many perish in the vast reaches of outer space, but many millions more survive and set up colonies. They take their place in the inter-galactic community. Sometimes they have to fight for survival. They learn how to do business. They learn the politics of co-existence. That's mankind two centuries from now, Henry."

She gives me a long stare.

"Nothing to say?"

"I've heard it before. It's the preamble to Level One."

"Correct. I wrote it. Every star system described in the game exists, every planet, every treaty, every war. You have to memorise them, Henry. The information could save your life."

She sees the way my mouth is hanging open.

"Now what?"

"Save my life? A game can't kill you."

Liesl rolls her eyes. "Do I have to go over it again, Henry? This isn't a game. I don't mean game dead. I mean dead dead, as in ex-human, the pile of ashes formerly known as Henry Kwok. Are you listening to me?"

I nod dumbly.

"The Three Heads of Cerberus is an inter-galactic conspiracy to destroy the uneasy peace that rules the stars. The game you've been playing is a training module based on the name of our enemy."

I'm still nodding, still dumbly.

"You don't get it, do you, Henry?"

I shake my head. No.

"Cerberus is a training manual. We are training you. You've been fighting Arden Xavier, the first head of Cerberus, but you've been doing it in the virtual world. A week from now you're going to do it for real."

"You're kidding."

Liesl shakes her head and leads me through a door. It appears seamlessly in the wall. We are now standing in a long tunnel. I glance at her, wondering what I'm supposed to do.

"Don't you recognise a shooting range when you see one?"

She places the flat of her palm on a glowing panel. It detaches from the wall and Liesl takes a familiar object from the recess.

"Is that the ZX90?"

"Do I need to answer that?"

I'm feeling stupid again. "No."

"Do you want to fire it?"

17

She hands me the lightweight weapon. I know its feel. I feel the twist grip on the barrel that will activate the Night Bloom. I hesitate.

"Something wrong?"

"I need those contact lenses."

"No, you don't. We're way past stuff like that. We programmed that feature into the game. Every time your retina encoded an image, we were programming it with the information you will need to operate the ZX90 to its full potential." She sees the doubtful frown. "Try it."

I turn to inspect my target. The far wall is now a crowd of Threnassic bug–men.

"You've been here before, Henry. You're on a crowded street. Arden Xavier is trying to make his escape. You've got one shot. Wing him. Take him alive. He is needed for interrogation."

This time there's no need for control gloves. I am physically inside the game. The street scene swarms around me. Liesl fades leaving me with the alien panorama. The virtual figures come rushing towards me. Instantly, I am on my toes, pounding on the moving track beneath my feet. I feel a new confidence running through me. I weave through the Threnassics, ducking, diving, peering this way and that. You wouldn't think it was possible, but I banish Liesl's watching, vivid blue eyes from my mind. It's just me and my quarry.

Then there he is, Arden Xavier. I steady myself, squeeze the trigger, use the computerised sight that prints itself on my retina and fire. Xavier yelps, claws at his shoulder with the pincers on his upper left arm. Got him! I run across, cuff each pair of arms. That's a lot of cuffing. Harsh light fills the room, banishing the virtual figures.

"Good work," Liesl says. "You were moving at high speed, but you kept your balance. You stayed focused and your shot was accurate. The real thing will be harder, much harder, but that was a decent dry run."

I'm beaming. I've spent most of the last half hour feeling totally inadequate. Suddenly I'm walking on air. I don't quite buy this woman-from-the-future, I-am-the-anointed-one, got-to-save-the-universe deal, but I also know there is nothing normal and everyday about this situation. I'm in the space between dream and reality and I love every minute of it.

"So where do I go from here?" I ask, still slightly breathless.

"When we've finished our business you go home," Liesl answers. "A week from now you go two hundred years in the future and half way across the universe to Thren 15 where they are hosting the Peace Conference."

"Yes, sure I do."

She gives me the hardest stare yet. "You're still not taking me seriously, are you?"

"Would you?" I counter. "I mean, I download a free computer game and the next thing I know somebody tells me I'm going to time travel into the future and save the universe."

"Don't big yourself up too much, Henry. You're a novice. You'll be part of a team."

"Will you be in it?" I ask, just a bit too eagerly.

She drops her eyes. "No, that can't happen."

I hear something in her voice, a big, heavy sadness like a stone.

"Something the matter?" I ask.

"I'm on Cerberus' wanted list. They've got my bio-rhythms. I step back in my own time and I'm dead within minutes."

"They track you by your bio-rhythms?" I ask.

"Got it in one. Cerberus is like a sophisticated Mafia, a state within a state. They've got the blood pressure, Body Mass Index, bone density, pH, cholesterol, every physical detail of their key opponents. They can lock on to their target in a matter of seconds, have a death squad tracking you in less than a minute. You'll be dead in ten. Max."

"Sounds like a computer game plot."

"This is no game, Henry. Why do you think I need you, a fourteen-year-old kid so wet behind the ears I could mop the floor with you?"

This I don't like. I'm tempted to sulk, but I don't.

"The bad guys don't have my bio-rhythms," I retort huffily.

"Hey, you're catching on. Correct."

"So why me? You've got seven billion people on this planet you could choose from. Why Henry Kwok?"

"Don't think we haven't tried others," Liesl tells me. "There have been better candidates, but they didn't want to play. Some refused to believe our offer. Some laughed in our face. Others were convinced, but didn't want to risk their necks."

Fine, I'm not your first choice. Way to put my nose out of joint, Schlachthof!

"So I'm not that special?"

"Oh, you're special, boy. When we go looking for a candidate for transportation we need somebody with the physical, mental and moral attributes to succeed."

This is more like it.

"Let's start with the transportation itself. You've got to have a certain level of fitness. No allergies. No hidden physical time bombs that could explode when we put you through the spacetime exchange. What we have is a complex nexus of factors. That narrows the group down to maybe ten thousand people on the whole planet."

"Ten thousand out of seven billion!"

"Correct."

I do the Maths.

"So I'm one in seventy thousand."

"That's right, Henry. You're special."

They're the kind of words I like to hear from the lips of the lovely Liesl. You're special.

Three

What Liesl Schlachthof told me in the games store next to the Noodles Bar on Wan Chai Road is harder to digest than the overcooked noodles. To send somebody into the future you need somebody fit. Which I am.

I do martial arts. I swim. I play tennis and football. I even do a bit of athletics. You need somebody with the precise balance of blood type, Body mass Index, resistance to allergies, cardio-vascular integrity, core cerebral balance, neuro-spatial endurance and a whole load of other stuff I didn't even try to understand. That's just getting your guinea pig through the wormhole. After that you need somebody in the top two to three per cent of academic ability in the population. I remember the grilling Liesl put me through.

Her: 199x34.

Me (after a few seconds): 6,766

Her: What is the boiling point of ethanol?

Me: 78 degrees centigrade.

Her: Name the seven stars in the Big Dipper.

Me: Dubhe, Merak, Phecda, Megrez, Alioth, Mizar and Alkaid.

Her: How do you treat the bite of a rabid Xentoroid Bull?

Me: How do you what now?

Her: Oh right, you haven't got that far in the game.

Me (not entirely seriously): So how *do you* treat the bite of a Xentoroid Bull?

Her: Rub with the crushed seedpod of a Prystyllis bush. Alternatively, you get somebody to pee on you at fifteen-minute intervals until the danger from the malignant pustules subsides.

Me (grimacing): I'll go with the Prystyllis bush, whatever that is.

Her: We need to step up your training.

I've had eight hours to sleep on my conversation with the gorgeous, mysterious, often glacial and always infuriatingly superior Liesl Schlachthof. I still don't know what to make of her and the things she tells me. Logically, it has to be some kind of elaborate scam. But what about the game? It's beyond state of the art. It's state of the art two centuries in the future. Then there's the simulation gallery and the ZX90. I've held it in my hand. This isn't some piece of computer kit. It's a weapon. OK, I'm no weapons expert, but the gun is real. I just know it.

Mum looks across the table at me.

"Are you OK?"

"Yes, why wouldn't I be?"

"You're very quiet."

I give her my pained look. "I can do quiet."

Anna pulls a face. "You can, but you don't."

I give her the evil eye. "And you do? You don't give yourself time to breathe."

That sets off a full-scale quarrel. Once Anna realises she isn't going to win she starts wailing.

"Mu-um!"

"Leave Anna alone," Mum tells me. "You're five years older, Henry. You should have more sense."

I think about arguing back, then I think about thinking about arguing back...and don't.

"You're in a funny mood."

There's no point protesting. I sit out breakfast, letting Anna's excited chatter wash over me. She's going to some party after school. Yardy yardy yar."

"What about you, Henry?"

I do a double take. "What?"

"Have you got any plans?"

"No, not really."

I'm about to say that I'm going to play Cerberus, but I think better of it.

"I've got an assignment to finish," I say. I don't sound too convincing, but Mum doesn't pick up on the slight hesitation.

"That's what I like to hear," Mum says. She glances at her watch. "I'm going to load the equipment for my presentation. Thanks for staying in for the delivery, by the way."

"Not a problem," I tell her.

Might as well clock up the Brownie points while I can.

"Anyway," Mum continues. "Priya's mum is going to pick Anna up for school then drop her back here. I'll be out until about eight o'clock. Are you OK with that?"

I'm more than OK with it. It means I'm going to be able to play Cerberus without Mum's prying eyes scrutinising everything I do.

I phone James. He's my alibi for the trip to Wan Chai Road so I'd better tell him.

"Can you cover for me?"

I explain without giving details. I'm bursting to tell him more. Before I can say another word he says he has something to tell me. That's a turn up.

"It's big," he says. "I mean, it's huge. It's life-changing."

OK, he's thrown down the challenge.

"I've got something to tell you too."

"Can't compare to my news," he says.

"Oh, I think it can."

"No way."

We're still playing this stupid game of one-upmanship when the intercom buzzes.

"I'll ring you back. Mum's home early."

"But, Henry, you have to hear my news. There's this girl."

"I'll ring you back."

"But, Henry."

I cut him off and press the intercom.

"Hello?"

"Buzz me in."

That voice. Husky. Feminine. Self-confident to the point of arrogance. It's Liesl. I'd know those silky, slightly European-accented tones anywhere.

"How do you know where I live?" I ask.

"Don't be obtuse, Henry," her voice crackles. "I know everything about you. Now let me in. I don't have all day."

I buzz her in and wait. Two minutes later she is standing in the doorway

23

wearing black and scarlet motorcycle leathers.

"You've got a bike."

"No," she says sarcastically. "I dress like this for fun."

I fume silently. Why, just once, can't she be nice to me?

"Aren't you going to invite me in?" she asks.

I step aside, still in a huff. You'd think she could be polite to me in my own home.

"I'm not stopping you," I say. "You don't need to be invited in. You're not a vampire. Or are you?"

She gives me the ice maiden stare. "You're in a funny mood."

"Why does everybody keep saying that?"

"Why, who's said it?"

"You. Mum."

"Your mum's a wise woman."

"She says that too."

That gets a laugh, which I like. Then there's a frown, which I don't like so much. It usually means I've done something wrong.

"Something the matter?"

She looks around and puts her helmet on the table.

"There's nothing wrong, but we have to speed things up. You've got to be ready to go in three days."

"Three days!"

"Correct."

"In three days you expect me to travel two hundred years into the future and half way across the universe and fight the scum of the skyways."

"Got it in one." She glances at my computer. "What level are you on?"

"Six."

"Then you're going to have to put in some serious game time." She considers the time scale. "If you complete three levels a day, you should be ready."

"Hang on right there," I say, holding my hands up. "You're going way too fast. This is a training manual, right?"

24

"Right."

"You expect me to remember hours of information just like that?"

Liesl gives me that pitying look. "Henry, you already did. When I say this is a training manual, I mean a training manual of a new kind. Everything you do on the game is instantly hardwired into your brain. Everything you experience in the game embeds itself into your subconscious brain. The things you do when you are playing become instinctive. It's like when somebody learns to touch-type. They can't tell you which letter is next to H..."

"G on one side, J on the other," I say helpfully.

That icy look again. "Quite. Anyway, as I was saying before I was so rudely interrupted, the typist may not be able to tell you which key is where, but once they place their fingers over the right keys they can type sixty words a minute. That's the way it was when you fired your first ZX90 assault rifle."

She's right. I knew exactly what to do. The weapon was part of me, like one of my own limbs.

"You're not dealing with any ordinary game here."

"I know, but that's impossible surely. Something like touch-typing takes time to learn. The game can't teach that quickly."

"It can, you know."

"You mean I do something once and I can do it every time?"

"Right, that's exactly what I mean, Henry."

I'm sceptical and that seems to royally bug her.

"You want me to prove it?" she demands.

OK, Ms Liesl Schlachthof, think you can bully me, do you? I face her down.

"I do."

She produces a greyish cylinder. "I thought you might need convincing. Do you recognise this?"

"Yes, it was in the last level I played. It's a Neutron Mine."

Liesl kneels down and places it on the floor. She primes it.

"OK," she says. "It's active. You've got sixty seconds to defuse it."

"Or?"

"Don't waste time, Henry. You know what will happen. 57 seconds."

I know what would happen in the game. The explosion would vapourise a square kilometre of the city. I go to work, glancing at Liesl a couple of times. She shows no sign of emotion. Suddenly, it is as if my hands are not my own. They remove the upper part of the casing. My fingers work on the circuit board. I locate the timer panel. It's all as easy as breathing and as involuntary. Hardwired. That was the word she used. Works for me.

"It's defused," I tell her.

"Did you find the parallel timer?"

"Of course."

"Good work, Henry."

"That was a fake, right?" I ask.

Liesl shakes her head. "No fake. This was the real deal."

"I don't believe you," I say. "No way would you bring a live bomb into the building. I mean, that would be crazy."

"Sometimes you have to be crazy to achieve great things."

"Did you get that from Wikiquote?"

She looks at me as if I've just crawled out of a crack in the wall.

"The peace of the universe is at stake, Henry. The device is real."

I stare at her for a few moments then I burst out laughing. "You nearly had me there."

Liesl glances at her watch. "How long before your mother and sister get home?"

"A couple of hours. Three hours max."

"Fine. We've got time. Come with me."

As I follow her to the lift I ask where we're going.

"You want proof the mine is real? You want a demonstration that this whole thing is genuine? I'll give you proof."

She leads the way to a gleaming Kawasaki Z750.

"Nice bike," I say approvingly.

She pops open the top box and hands me a helmet.

"Jump on."

I look at her sleek back and I can almost forgive her the constant stream of criticism. I'm barely seated when she takes off, weaving in and out of the busy traffic. It's a hair-raising ride. The city streets flash by. I cling on tightly, loving the feel of my hands on her waist. I recognise Tuen Mun Road. Before long we arrive at a marina. Liesl looks round at me.

"You can take your hands off my waist now."

Can.

Don't want to.

She shoves me off my seat and hauls the bike up on its stand. I give her a questioning look.

"This is it," she says.

I look around, wondering what we're doing at a marina and yacht club.

"No," she says, seeing my confusion. "*This* is it."

I'm staring at a gleaming, white speedboat, the kind James Bond would choose.

"You like?"

"I *like*!"

She dangles a key under my nose. "Let's go."

Soon we're skipping across the waves. She turns to look at me.

"Fast enough?"

I laugh. "No way. Go faster."

She grins. "I was hoping you'd say that."

She pulls a lever. What happens next isn't fast. It's insane. Water is hitting my face like a swarm of hornets. The wind is a razor cutting at my flesh. Liesl shouts something, but I can't hear her. I cup my hand behind my ear. She leans closer. I can smell her perfume, feel the warmth of her cheek. I'm suffering GGO – that's Gorgeous Girl Overload.

"Fast enough?"

I nod, wide-eyed.

She leans even closer. Her lips brush my ear, which makes my skin burn with embarrassment. At least, I think it's embarrassment.

"Hold the wheel. Look out for shipping. You kill the pair of us and I will be seriously disappointed."

Funny lady. Not! I stare at the open sea in front of me. I can hear strange, metallic clanks behind me. She is erecting some kind of device.

"What are you doing?"

There's no answer. I chance a look backwards and my jaw drops. She's assembled something that looks like a mortar. She sees me staring and yells.

"Keep your eyes on the sea!"

I turn back, see an oncoming vessel and swing the wheel. What's she up to? After a few moments, she taps my shoulder and takes over. She jerks a thumb at the mortar-like device.

"Watch."

A red light is flickering on the side. It flickers faster and faster. She's loaded the Neutron Mine into the launcher. She's reactivated it and now she's going to fire it into the air. There's a loud pop and the Neutron Mine streaks into the sky. It climbs and climbs until it is out of sight then there is a loud thud. The air ripples and we are struck by a powerful shock wave that makes the sea boil around us. Half a dozen fish float to the surface, quite dead.

"Still think I wouldn't take a live device into the block?" she asks, turning the boat.

"Are you insane?" I cry. "What if it had gone off?"

"I knew that wouldn't happen," she said.

"You trust me that much?" I ask.

She laughs. "I trust the game. I trust our ability to train you to the optimum level."

I wonder what she means by *our* ability. She says *we* a lot, but there is no sign of anyone else being involved in this whole affair.

"Are you OK with all this, Henry? You look like you sucked a lemon."

"I'm OK."

"Well, if anything bothers you, call me." She hands me her cellphone number. "Any time night or day."

It takes twenty minutes to reach the marina. It takes half an hour to reach my apartment block. Lisa takes the helmet from me.

"You'd better get upstairs," she says. "That's your mum coming now."

She's right. I'm riding the lift when I realise that not only does she know where I live. She also knows what every member of my family looks like. The game's for real. The mission's for real.

Un-be-lieve-ab-le!

Four

Why me? I mean, why me, Henry Kwok, International School student, more or less ordinary kid even if my grades are off-the-scanner, well-kick-me-in-the-head-aren't-you-clever brilliant. I thought people only woke up sweating in the movies, but here I am, at three o'clock in the morning, lying awake with beads of perspiration on my forehead in spite of the aircon. This can't be real. OK, I've seen all this stuff with my own eyes. It can't be anything other than real. But time travel, being transported through a wormhole? That's nuts.

There's this other thing. I can't get it out of my head. How can I just go off on some mind-blowing adventure and leave my family? They'll think I've been kidnapped, or worse. I remember what Liesl said. Call me. Any time, night or day. OK, you said it, blue eyes. Here goes. I grab my cellphone and duck under the duvet to muffle the sound of conversation. I thumb her number into the keypad. After a couple of minutes there's her voice, loud and clear, sleep falling away.

"What is it, Henry?"

"I can't just vanish off the face of the Earth. My mum and dad will go crazy."

"They won't know you're gone."

"Of course they'll know I'm gone."

"No, Henry, they won't. You don't read much science fiction, do you?"

"A bit."

"How much?"

"Not that much."

"Any at all?"

I grunt an admission of defeat.

"None."

"Let's make it simpler. Do you watch *Friends*?"

"I catch the re-runs on cable sometimes. Why?"

"Do you remember the play Joey was in? He climbs up the ladder into a spaceship. He tells his girlfriend she will grow old while he is away, but he won't age at all. He says for her to tell her granddaughter about him."

The answer is vague.

"Why are you telling me this?"

Liesl sighs. "Because, Henry, there is an element of truth in Joey's story. Time can warp, twist. That's part of the way a wormhole works. Best guess estimate, you will be gone ten days. Less than a second will elapse in this time. We've done the calculations on this. Trust me."

"That's impossible."

"It's entirely possible. In fact, that's the way it is. Go to sleep, Henry. You're no good to us exhausted."

She hangs up. I lie there with the glow of the phone on my face then it dims leaving me with the darkness and my thoughts. I'm going into the future. I toss and turn, my head swarming with all the crazy things that have happened since Cerberus came into my life. My thoughts ratchet back and forth. One moment I'm convinced it's real, the next I tell myself it's got to be some kind of elaborate scam. But I know it isn't. What happened with the Neutron Mine, how could that be faked? It just isn't possible.

The time crawls by. The scarlet digits on the face of my alarm clock just sit there, refusing to change. I twist this way and that, trying to bury my thoughts and fears in the pillow, but nothing I do brings me any closer to sleep. Eventually I get up and start to play on Cerberus. I get through two more levels before my eyelids start to droop. Finally I sleep.

But I don't sleep long. There is a strange tapping noise then I am staring at the alarm clock. It is 4.30. Weird, I think, what was that tapping I dreamed about? Then there it is again: tap, tap, tap. This time I am wide awake. It is coming from the window. I swing my legs out of bed, scramble into my clothes and pad across to the window in my bare feet. I open the blinds and gasp. It's Liesl. She's outside my bedroom window. "But that's impossible," I say out loud. "We're on the eleventh floor."

She mouths something. I don't understand. We've got double-glazed windows. I frown. She shakes her head and makes a gesture. It says: let me in. The second gesture seems kind of rude. I slip into the living room quietly and turn the key to the door that leads onto the balcony. Liesl makes her way inside. She doesn't look happy at being left outside while I struggled out of my deep sleep. I lead the way into my room.

"What are you doing here?' I whisper.

"It's time."

"Time for what?"

She makes with the big eyes as if I am the stupidest boy in the universe.

"No way. You said we'd got days."

"The wormhole is unstable. We've had to revise our calculations twice already. We've got a brief window of access to the spacetime continuum. If we miss this opportunity goodness knows when we'll get another one."

"But I'm not ready. I've got two levels of the game to go."

"That's a risk we'll have to take. You've got most of the base skills and you'll get help on the other side."

"I thought this Cerberus network had your people under surveillance."

"That's right. If any of them tried to tail Xavier they would be dead in minutes. That doesn't mean they can't help you."

I do my dumb boy nod then something occurs to me.

"How did you get up here? Some kind of gizmo from the future?"

Liesl shakes her head. "Nothing that sophisticated. I hoisted myself up on the window cleaner's cradle." She slips off her backpack. She unzips it slowly to cut down on the noise. "Take these."

She hands me three circular, metal discs. One nearly slips from my grasp.

"Hold them tightly, you idiot!"

I give her a hard stare. Who's she calling an idiot?

"The discs are calibrated to your bio-rhythms. If you accidentally reset one of them your arrival could be thrown fifty years out." She points at the floor. "Set them out in a triangle."

I do as she says. This time I am really careful. She seems to approve. Satisfied with my efforts, she produces what looks like a square torch. She turns the beam towards the ceiling and presses a button. Instantly, three beams of sapphire light radiate from the central point on the ceiling.

"Make sure each beam of light lines up with the dimple in the middle of the discs."

I shuffle the discs around the carpet until all three beams are locked into place. Liesl seems satisfied and hits another button. Now there is a translucent, sapphire pyramid pulsating in the middle of my room.

"Take your clothes off," she says.

"What?"

"Strip. You can leave your boxers on."

Big of her!

"Why've I got to strip off?"

Liesl shakes her head. "See that belt?"

I nod.

"Metal buckle. In the spacetime transfer, it could fuse with your internal organs."

"That sounds bad."

"The buckle would melt into your liver and kidneys."

"Definitely bad."

Liesl draws a finger across her throat. "As in death is bad."

"The watch."

"Uh huh?"

"It would tighten like a garotte, cut off your circulation. You could lose the hand. You don't have any fillings do you."

I shake my head. "I've got good teeth."

"Good. I would have had to remove them."

"You're kidding!"

"When the peace of the universe is at stake, I don't do jokes." She reads a display on the torch. "Get into the pyramid."

"That's it? I get in and go?"

"What do you expect, a marching band and ticker tape parade? You've played Cerberus, Henry. You should be acclimatised to the environment on the other side. When you arrive, your contact will be waiting for you. He's a Somnolent called Yrin Gok. Do as he says."

"Will he have some clothes for me?"

She gives me a *well d'uh* look. I don't even ask her to explain what a Somnolent is.

"OK, sorry I asked."

I sit cross-legged in the pyramid. My heart is pounding. What the hell am I doing? Liesl hits another button and the sapphire light plays around me, moulding itself to the contours of my body. I feel a tickling sensation all over my skin, but nothing unpleasant or scary. That settles my nerves a little, but the sense of well-being doesn't last long. Within seconds my heart begins to race. My pulse and heartbeat go into overdrive. What's happening to me? I give Liesl a startled look. For the first time she shows me some kind of sympathy, holding out her palms to reassure me.

My heartbeat slows. I glance at Liesl, wondering what to expect. Within seconds I am shivering. I am so cold the shock takes my breath away. My skin is numb. I feel listless, barely able to keep my eyes open. That's

33

when I feel the first jolt. It is as if an invisible fist has punched me in the stomach. I gasp. Another invisible fist thuds into my kidneys. Soon the ghost blows are raining down on me, pounding me to a pulp. I want to scream, but even now I am aware of Mum and Anna asleep across the landing. I close my eyes and concentrate on keeping silent. When I reopen them, the room has vanished, Liesl too. What now?

The answer comes within seconds. Wave after wave of sapphire light is rushing at me, accelerating. I know I am still sitting on the carpet. I can feel it against my skin. But there is no carpet, no room. There is no apartment building. There is just me. I am a rock and deep-blue waves of light are breaking over me. It is a few moments before I realise that I am warm. The ribbons of light are bathing me, soothing away the earlier hammer blows. The waves continue to speed up, the gaps between them becoming ever shorter. Then the process goes into reverse. They are slowing, slowing. When the sapphire glow finally clears I am sitting in an alleyway. It is alien yet familiar. I know this place from the game. I am on the other side. I am two hundred years in the future. OK, this isn't Terminator. I'm not naked, but I'm not far off. Where the hell is this Somnolent guy? Where's Yrin Gok?

Now this can't be good. As far as I know I am two hundred years in the future, barefoot, standing shivering in my boxer shorts and feeling about as stupid as a fourteen-year-old Chinese kid can feel. OK, I have a mission, a great destiny, I am the dude who is going to save the universe, but right now I am cold and embarrassed and lost.

"Yrin Gok," I hiss, "where the hell are you?"

"I'm here."

I start with surprise. Yrin has crept up behind me and tapped my shoulder.

"How did you do that?" I demand. "I didn't hear you coming."

Yrin isn't quite what I expected. He is two and a half metres tall and is dressed from head to foot in scarlet robes. His skin is snow white. His long, braided crimson hair tumbles over broad shoulders. He has deep-wine-red eyes that match his robes.

"Nobody hears me coming," Yrin says proudly. "I am a Warmaster. My hands are lethal killing machines. My feet are deadly weapons. My..."

He doesn't finish the sentence. The next moment he is lying crumpled on the ground, snoring loudly.

"Yrin," I say, shaking him by the shoulder. "Yrin?"

He shrugs me away and carries on talking as if nothing has happened.

"...eyes are laser beam darts of terror." He stops talking. "Oh, did I do it again?"

"You fell asleep. One moment you were chattering away, the next you were fast asleep on the ground. What gives?"

"That's the problem with us Somnolents. We are great warriors, feared across the starways, but we do have this unfortunate tendency to...doze off."

"And it can happen at any time?"

"Yes."

"In the middle of a fight?"

"Yes."

"Isn't that dangerous?"

"Very," Yrin confirms. "In many a great battle, when the outcome lay in the balance, our fighters have fallen asleep and been slain where they lay. It is the tragedy of our condition. We are the greatest of fighters and the most piteous of creatures. My own father drowned in the Gambeddle soup he was eating."

His eyes well with tears. I don't ask what Gambeddle is.

"Is there nothing you can do?"

Yrin shakes his head.

"Nothing. Since the night of the Great Aurora the Somnolent race has suffered this dread affliction."

"So instead of ruling the universe..."

"We sleep through the key moments of history. I was invited to the President's first term inauguration and slept right through it."

35

"Bummer."

"Quite." He stares down the alley, lost in thought. "Anyway, there is no time to dwell on the problems of five million Somnolents in a bleak, cruel universe. I have but a few minutes before Cerberus becomes suspicious. I must return to my normal routine or one of its agents will come looking for me. I am under almost constant surveillance. I..."

He starts to sink to the ground, eyelids drooping.

"Yrin," I say, holding him up. "Yrin!"

His eyes flutter open. "What? Oh, sorry." He shakes his head in an attempt to clear his senses. "Here are your clothes. Get dressed. Do you remember your first contact point from the game."

"Yes, I am to proceed to a breakfast bar in the district of Brizenhoff."

Yrin hands me a ring. "You wear it this way round," he explains. "I have downloaded ten thousand credits from various companions. Place your palm on the reader in any retail outlet and it will pay for anything you need, rooms, food, clothing, entertainment, travel. You should have more than enough to purchase anything you need."

A siren wails across Brizenhoff.

"I have to go. If I am not at my work station in half an hour Cerberus will put a tail on me."

"Cerberus is that powerful?"

"Cerberus is a state within a state. It is on the verge of power. But for the President, it would rule the planets already."

I watch him hurry away. He crumples to the ground at the top of the alley, dozes for about ten seconds then continues on his way. So that is Yrin Gok, definitely the strangest person I have ever met and that includes my sister Anna. I make my way to the breakfast bar. Thanks to the game, the streets are familiar. I watch the skyways swarming with silent skyflitters. The streets below are run down. Neon lights blaze through the rising steam from the heating gratings. The future isn't the shiny paradise I had always imagined.

I move quickly. Neither the cops in their black uniforms nor the passers-

by pay me the slightest attention. I force myself not to stare. For the first time I am seeing the Threnassics in the flesh, hurrying bug-men. There are many other life forms, tall, loping Hoopwots, hunchbacked, fire-breathing Meeners, sinister, translucent Skellits. I've encountered every one of them as I trawled through the levels of the game. It takes the edge off their unfamiliarity. I pass for one more itinerant traveller on the great trading planet Thren 15.

The game has begun.

Five

I try not to stare at the twin suns of Thren 15 rising over the rooftops. If I want to be accepted as a traveller who belongs to this time and this place, I have to look upon sights like this with a casual disregard. I walk into the breakfast bar. Cerberus has prepared me well. I recognise the oval tables, the rough, stone counter, the manager, an Azaal woman in traditional robe and veil. The veil is like nothing on Earth. There is no eye slit and the material is opaque. The Azaals are eyeless. They negotiate their surroundings using their own natural sonar. The manager hears me enter, identifies me by bouncing sound waves off me.

"Ah, a humanoid visitor," she says. "We don't get many of you round here. What would you like to eat?"

I pick up the menu. The game has prepared me to read Azaala, the printed Azaal language.

"I might have Azaal Flakes," I think out loud.

"Would you like them live or dead?" she asks.

I realise the game hasn't prepared me as thoroughly as I thought. I don't like the sound of living food. My gaze races down the menu looking for something familiar. I settle on sweet Manu bread in pink grape sauce.

"Not the Azaal Flakes, then? That's what he's having."

I follow her gaze and see a Hoopwot space cruiser captain hoovering up a bowlful of green beetles with his prehensile snout. He sees me looking.

"Delicious," he declares.

I force a smile as he crunches the carapaces and slurps the goo within.

"I'll take your word for it."

There are only three customers. There is the Hoopwot in the corner. There is a Threnassic businessman sitting in a booth by the door. He's watching the news on a 3-D hologram broadcast. I am the third. I know what to do to pull up my own news flash. I reach out, holding my hand over a purple disc on the floor and raise my arm quickly. The gesture pulls up a column of light that forms into the same kind of 3-D hologram the Threnassic is watching.

"Now back to our headline item," the news anchor announces. "Delegations are arriving from all over the galaxy for the start of the Third Biennial Peace Conference. Most commentators believe this is the most crucial inter-planetary conference in a generation. Tensions are growing between the Democratic Federation and the Expansion Alliance. The Expansionists are demanding the right to occupy the uninhabited Free Planetary Belt. They argue that the Belt is in their area of influence. The DF insists that the Belt is a necessary peace line and that must remain uninhabited and neutral."

They may as well be speaking a foreign language for all I understand. A familiar face appears.

"President Krenatki Shavlotan will open the conference tomorrow. Security is tight around the conference centre."

There is film of Threnassic State Police sweeping the areas surrounding the conference centre for bombs. I recognise every street, every walkway. This is where I tracked Arden Xavier in the game. At that moment the door opens and a Meener walks in. Flames are licking round his leathery lips. I can feel the heat of his fiery breath four metres away. He sees President Shavlotan's image flickering away.

"That peacemonger," he snarls. "If he has his way we'll all be sitting with flowers in our hair instead of exploiting the possibilities of the Belt."

I am tempted to point out that the Meener doesn't actually have any hair, but I think better of it.

The Threnassic looks up. "Shavlotan's right, blow-breath. You Expansionists will never be satisfied. It's the Belt today, the Threnassic Zone tomorrow. All you want is interstellar domination."

The Meener snarls angrily. "Who asked your opinion, bug-boy?"

The Threnassic springs to his feet. "Take that back."

They are squaring up. Before either of them can land a blow, the manager takes a weapon down from the wall.

"Take a step back, gentlemen," she warns them. "The first one who starts something gets his head blown off."

"You're bluffing," the Meener sneers.

The manager points the plasma rifle at a spot between his eyes.

"Try me," she says. "Go on, sucker. Make my day. A splash of Meener blood on that wall would be quite a talking point."

The Meener thinks better of it and lumbers over to the door. "Fine, I'll take my custom somewhere else."

"You do that," says the manager. "I don't want to see your raggedy ass in my place again, hotlips."

The manager puts my Manu bread in front of me. I pick up a spoon, drench the first mouthful in grape sauce and put it in my mouth. Instantly the sweetness explodes on my tongue."

"Wow!"

"Good?" she asks.

"Delicious. Mouths were made for this moment."

She cocks her head. "You'd think you'd never had Manu bread before."

The Threnassic gives me a long, enquiring stare. I realise I've got to be more careful. He could be a Cerberus agent. I remember the galaxy's recent history. President Shavlotan is pursuing a peace strategy. The Expansion Alliance has hooked up with Cerberus, the shadowy inter-planetary Mafia, to undermine his Presidency. They have a common aim. They want to end the uneasy peace of the last half-century and unleash a war of conquest. If their plan is to succeed, Shavlotan must die. That is where I come in. My job is to take out Arden Xavier before he can put a power bolt in Shavlotan's head. One problem. I'm waiting for the guy who is going to take me to the ZX90 assault rifle I need for the job. I wait. And wait. And wait.

"Another Manu bread?" the manager asks.

"No thanks," I answer.

"Something to drink then?"

I nod.

"What will it be?"

"Surprise me."

I can't see her face, but there is a smile in her voice when she says OK. Two minutes later I understand why she suggested a drink. The glass comes with a coaster. I take a sip of my drink and notice that there is something on the coaster. It looks like an earplug. I slip it into my ear. Immediately, the manager's voice fills my head. I glance at the customers who have entered in the last few minutes. Nobody can hear but me.

"I'm Azari Azaal, your contact. Don't turn round."

I keep my gaze fastened on the street.

"In five minutes my sister will walk past the window. She will be wearing emerald robes like me. Don't acknowledge her. Follow at a discreet distance. She will lead you to the weapon. Remove the plug and drop it in the glass. It will dissolve. Oh, and don't drink from it. It's acid."

Now she tells me! I could have drunk that! I do as she says. Presently, I see the sister walking by and fall in behind her. She walks quickly and purposefully. I have to hurry to keep up. We enter a seedier part of the city. The lights are dimmer, the inhabitants grubbier and more suspicious. I notice a Somnolent arguing with a couple of Meeners. He dozes off in mid-sentence and they go through his pockets, stealing his money. I want to stop, but the sister is almost out of sight. I hurry after her.

She turns left into a dark, winding alleyway. She is almost out of sight when she flicks out her right hand pointing into a doorway. I jog down to the place she indicated. It is a workshop. It specialises in skyflitter repairs. I glance at the owner, a gloomy-looking Threnassic. He is using all his pairs of pincers to repair three different vehicles. He talks to me without looking up.

"Your order's in the back, sir."

I make my way through the cluttered interior, stepping over space drives and retro rockets, landing gear and asteroid shields, pulse cannons and thorium processors. I am about to ask for help when I see a backpack labelled: 'to be collected.' I tug at the fastening. It's the stripped-down ZX90. The Threnassic stamps past me.

"You OK assembling it?"

"Yes, I've had training."

"Leave through the other door. I don't want anybody getting curious."

I nod and walk briskly through the front door onto the street. I am acutely aware that I'm lugging a stripped-down assault rifle. In the heightened atmosphere around the Peace Conference I could be stopped at any time. The streets are swarming with police units. I would be hard pushed to explain what I was doing with an assassin's weapon such as the ZX90. I force myself to maintain a steady pace. I'm determined not to attract attention.

I know where I'm going. Cerberus contained a route to my accommodation. I make my way to the Crater B&B. There is an automated check-in. I pass the credit ring over the reader. The machine coughs out a small piece of paper. It is the code for my room. I take the lift to the twentieth floor and tap the number into the keypad outside room 2001. The room works by voice recognition.

"Chair," I say.

A chair slides out of the wall.

"Table."

The table follows.

"Mini bar."

A panel slides back and I take a can of fizz. I gaze out of the window, sipping from the can. Two centuries on and they haven't found a better way of packaging drinks. I am astonished that, no matter how many amazing changes I witness, in so many ways the future isn't that different to the world I left. I can see the Presidential Palace and the conference centre where Xavier will try to assassinate Shavlotan. It's the strangest thing but, even though I have only been here for a day and some of the things I see are kind of unreal, I feel right at home. Cerberus the game has done its job well, introducing me to the hurricane of new sights and sounds. Cerberus the conspiracy is out there planning to let loose the dogs of war. I hear a sound. It is the opening theme of the game.

"Computer," I say.

A robotic arm plants a wafer-thin unit on the table. I stand in front of it the way Liesl showed me and I tap in the word: receive. Liesl's face appears on the screen.

"You made it then?"

"Yes, I made it." I allow myself a bit of bravado. "Piece of cake."

"How are you settling in?"

"Fine, I've got the...." I hesitate. "Is this a secure communication?"

"It's encrypted. Nobody can hear us."

"I've got the gun," I say.

"Excellent." She seems genuinely impressed that I made all my contacts. "Get yourself some sleep, Henry. It's a big day tomorrow. The peace of the universe is in your hands."

Then she's gone. She's right. I should sleep.

"Chair go," I say.

It slides into the wall.

"Table go."

Ditto.

"Computer go. Mini bar go."

Now the room is clear.

"Bed," I say.

The bed appears and I drop onto it. It isn't even lunchtime, but I need a nap. My mind is racing. Part of me says I belong here. The game has done its job. I move easily around Thren 15. Another part of me reminds me that I'm a fourteen-year-old kid and screams that I am out of my depth. Exhaustion kicks in and my mind slows. In a matter of minutes I am fast asleep.

Six

A loud, buzzing noise wakes me. I sit up, disoriented, still trying to work out where I am. I hear a voice.

"Let me in."

It's Yrin Gok. I stumble to the door, rubbing my eyes. Suddenly, every time I sleep somebody comes knocking.

"I thought you had to stay away from me," I say. "You know, bio-rhythms and all that."

Yrin gives the corridor a furtive glance.

"Sometimes you have to throw caution to the winds," he says.

"What gives?"

"There's something wrong."

Now my skin is prickling. Don't tell me something's wrong. Tell me everything's right.

"Explain."

"I wish I could, young Kwok. It's just a feeling."

So speak to me, old Gok.

"Sofa," I say.

We sit down. I am starting to gather my thoughts. I glance at Yrin's troubled face.

"You've got to give me more than a feeling," I say.

Yrin continues to look worried. "I wish I could. Take it from a Gok to a Kwok. Something doesn't match up here. Who recruited you?"

"Her name is Liesl Schlachthof."

"Schlachthof? The name doesn't mean anything to me."

My scalp tingles. What's happening here? Surely the saviours of the universe should be aware of each other. I ask a question.

"So how did you get involved?"

"One of my brother Somnolents said there was going to be an attempt on the President's life."

"You trust this guy?"

"I did." There's a look in his eyes that makes me more concerned than ever. "He's dead. They found him in an alley with his brains blown out."

Suddenly I am as anxious as my crimson-haired friend. First, he's never heard of Liesl Schlachthof then one of his comrades is murdered. Something stinks to high heaven and I don't mean the Azaal Flakes.

"Yrin..."

I don't get to finish my sentence. He's dozed off and is face down on the sofa."

"Yrin. Yrin?"

He stirs himself.

"What time is it?"

"Still six in the evening. You've only been out for a few seconds. No need to worry."

He shakes his head fiercely. "There is every reason to worry, young Kwok. We have both been drawn into a conspiracy. Tomorrow you will walk into a security hotspot looking for one of the most expert assassins in the galaxy."

"You know Xavier?"

"I know *of* him....or her. Arden Xavier is something of a mystery."

"That's not true. He's a Threnassic. We know that much."

Yrin hesitates.

"What's wrong?"

"I don't know who's given you this information. I have seen wanted posters on a thousand screens across the starways. On some he is humanoid. On others he is a Meener. On still others he is a Hoopwot. I have seen a score of representations of our friend Arden Xavier, but there is no concrete evidence he even exists. He has no criminal record. He has never done time. Tracking down Arden Xavier is like chasing a shadow."

"*I've* seen him," I say.

"You have!"

I explain about Cerberus the game. I describe the training sessions, the hastily glimpsed images of Xavier.

"One piece of advice," Yrin says. "Trust nobody."

"Not even you?"

He corrects himself. "That would be preposterous. Trust nobody *except* me. I am a warrior of unimpeachable honour."

He glances at the time.

"I've got to go. If I'm not seen at any of my usual haunts in the next couple of minutes there will be a Cerberus agent on my tail."

I realise that he does actually have a tail. I hear him hurrying down the corridor to the lift.

"TV," I say.

The news is covering the delegates' arrival in Thren 15. I watch the different alien races. Some of them wave to the cameras. Others do interviews on the spot. Still others stand frozen-faced, considering the scene before them. Yrin's visit has got me worried. If only I could contact Liesl and reassure myself, but I don't know how. I have to wait for the familiar theme tune. It isn't long before I'm climbing the walls. I stand at the window looking out across the city. I make my decision.

"Safe."

I stow the ZX90 in the safe and set off to explore the streets around the hotel. As the twin suns set over the roofs the district comes to life. Night races in like a swarm of flies. Lights stutter to life in the gloom. There are street stalls selling clothes, food and all kinds of gadgets. I stop to watch a party of Hoopwot tourists crowding round a live food stall. They are soon hoovering up a wide range of bugs, worms, snakes and unspeakable crustaceans. Within moments I am feeling quite sick.

I come across a kind of Speakers' Corner. It is divided equally between supporters of the Expansionists and the Democratic Federation. The speeches become more heated. It isn't long before there is a pitched battle between the Meeners on one side and the bug-like Threnassics on the other. The police arrive and start bundling the fighting groups into the back of hover vans. The Chief of Police uses a loud hailer to order the crowd to disperse. I am still watching the mayhem when I notice a familiar face observing from a shop-lined piazza. It's Azari Azaal. I find myself frowning and remember Yrin Gok's concern that something is wrong. Could it have something to do with Azari Azaal? I hope not. I like her. I decide to follow her. Soon I am weaving in and out of the bustling crowds, squinting through the steam from the food stalls. The crowds thin and I find myself on a deserted street. Azari stops and slips through a door into a domed building made entirely of emerald glass. Once she is safely inside I edge up the wall and try to peer inside. The glass is opaque. I make my way to the door and ease it open. Through the gap I can see a gathering. Everyone, male or female, is dressed in emerald robes. It is a temple.

After a few moments I hear footsteps and somebody approaches. I slip away and duck down in the shadows. The Azaal looks up and down the street and locks the door. I rack my brains. Cerberus didn't prepare me for this. I wander round the perimeter of the glass temple, but there is no way in. I am still wondering what to do when I see dark outlines in the sky. The shadowy forms approach silently. It is a fleet of police skyflitters. They mass over the roof of the glass temple. For a moment they hang in the air then, in unison, they activate their searchlights. The light is brighter than phosphorus.

Instantly, assault units abseil from the skyflitters and surround the building. I shrink back into a recess. The crack police units set charges and blow the door before swarming into the temple. Within moments the first of the Azaals is being led, hands on head, from the building. One protests that it was a peaceful gathering. The nearest cop, a huge

Threnassic wearing a bulletproof vest, drives his rifle butt into the protesting Azaal's stomach. I spot Azari at the back of the line. She starts to struggle, setting off furious resistance. In the confusion, she breaks free and races back towards the city centre pursued by an armed Threnassic. I follow at a discreet distance.

The Threnassic is gaining on Azari when she turns and leaps into the air, her spangled slipper crashing between his bug eyes. The cop staggers back, dropping his weapon. He is getting to his feet when Azari pumps her fist into his face. Once, twice, three times in quick succession. She stands there panting. I take advantage of the moment and grab the cop's gun.

"OK, Azari, what was all that about?"

She sees that I've got the drop on her.

"You!"

"That's right, me, Henry Kwok, the kid who likes answers. Why are the cops after you and the other Azaals? Have you got anything to do with Cerberus?"

"Yes, Henry, I've got a lot to do with Cerberus."

I am shocked by her honesty.

"I'm fighting it, you young fool."

"So why are the police after you?"

"You think I'm involved in the attempt to assassinate the President?"

"Aren't you?"

The cop is starting to stir.

"I think we should discuss this elsewhere," Azari suggests.

I'm in a dilemma. Do I go with her or shop her to the police? I have to make a decision. I give her the benefit of the doubt. I disarm the weapon and go with her.

"OK, where now?"

"I know somewhere."

She leads me to a street of doors. That's it. Just doors. She pays her credits and one of the doors opens.

"Well, don't just stand there. The cops will be looking for us."

I follow her down a narrow passage to a small room with a table and two chairs.

"What is this place?"

"A registry office."

"We're getting married?"

"Don't be silly, Henry. We're not going to activate the ceremony. At least we can talk without being overheard. These places rely on confidentiality."

"So it's a kind of automated Gretna Green?"

I can't see her face, but I know she's confused.

"Why did the police raid the glass temple?" I demand.

"You mean you don't know? Who are you, Henry Kwok? What's behind the name? What makes you tick?"

My neck burns. Cerberus has left me with major gaps in my knowledge. Maybe the missing levels were more important than I thought.

"I'll tell you my story sometime," I tell her. "Right now you're the one doing the explaining."

"A few years ago the Azaal council made a big mistake. It decided to back the Expansionists. Our leaders staged a rising against the government. My father led a movement to change the council's policy. He paid with his life, but most Azaals now support the President. The police haven't forgotten the rebellion. They see us as a dangerous, terrorist movement."

"And you're not?"

Suddenly, I don't trust anybody. What if the police are right? What if she's part of the Cerberus conspiracy? What if I'm about to be fed to the lions?

"You've got to believe me, Henry? All I want is peace. The temple gathering was discussing how we can regain the trust of the people of Thren 15."

I stand up.

"I don't know what to believe. It's all so complicated. Who do I trust?

48

You know what, I wish I could get out of this place and go home."

"And where's home, Henry?"

I head for the door.

"Wouldn't you like to know?"

She tries to call me back, but I keep on going, down the passage, onto the street and into the night. The question flashes through my mind a second time. Who do I trust? Who is telling me the truth? Is it her, Yrin, Liesl or is it none of the above? I've got some thinking to do.

I do the thinking. It doesn't help. Sometimes you do the thinking and things become clearer. I've spent the whole evening doing the thinking and I just keep thinking the same thing: I don't know what to think. I have thought myself into a corner where I don't know who my friends are, who my enemies are, what I'm doing here. Nothing is simple. There are good Hoopwots and bad Hoopwots, good Threnassics and bad Threnassics. It is probably the same for the other races on this planet. I'm confused. I'm scared. I want somebody to tell me what to do.

I hear the Cerberus theme and scramble over to the computer screen. There's Liesl on the screen, blue eyes clear and calm. She'll know what to do.

"How's it going, Henry?"

"Things aren't going to plan, Liesl."

I tell her what Yrin said. I tell her about Azari and the assault on the glass temple.

"It's all so confusing. I can't tell the good guys from the bad guys. It's not like a game any more."

Liesl is as calm and collected as ever. "Henry, it isn't a game. It never was a game." She sounds rattled. It's unsettling. She is usually so cool, so superior. What's changed? "You want to know why it's confusing? You've stepped into the middle of the biggest crisis to hit the galaxy in half a century. This is for real, Henry. It's happening and you're part of it."

I'm part of it. "Fine, Liesl. What does that mean?"

"You've got the weapon, right?"

More anxiety in her voice. I do my best to reassure her.

"Yes, it's in the safe."

"Good. That's good. Very good."

"Why's it good?"

"It's good, Henry Kwok, because your mission hasn't changed. Tomorrow you make your way to the inauguration. The ZX90 is made of Metakyprosium, an element found only on Metakal in the Lycan-Thyperidean asteroid belt."

I'm thinking it's made of what found on the where in the what, but she keeps on talking.

"It is light, efficient and completely undetectable by the police scanners. You work your way down to the central security cordon and take out Arden Xavier before he can shoot the President."

"But why me, Liesl? None of this makes any sense. Why pluck a fourteen-year-old kid from Hong Kong to carry out the most important job in the galaxy? I've been sleepwalking into this madness and I just don't get it."

Liesl talks slowly. She reminds me of my unique combination of mental and physical skills and biological make-up.

"I'm a kid!" I yell. "How am I supposed to save the life of the President?"

"You know how," Liesl says, still quiet, still measured, still calm. "You are perfectly equipped for the task. Cerberus has trained you."

"Yes sure, the magic computer game that can programme me to fight the conspiracy of the same name."

"Exactly. Don't go crazy on me now, Henry."

I drop my head.

"Look at me, Henry." She raises her voice. "Henry, look at me! You're the only one standing between the people of the galaxy and all-out war. You've got to do this. It's your duty."

I take a deep breath. "OK, I'll do it."

"Sure?"

"Sure."

"I love you, Henry Kwok."

Did she just say she loves me?

"You can do this. You're good."

I nod. "Yes, I'm good."

"Hang on in there, Henry Kwok," she says, a smile on her full, red lips. "Get some sleep. You've got a big job tomorrow. Go save the universe." I lose the link. Yes sure, go save the universe. I try to get some sleep. I try. I fail. Maybe it's because I had a nap this afternoon. More likely it's because my mind's racing with everything that's happened and everything that's going to happen. Maybe it's because the most gorgeous woman I have ever seen just said she loved me. I see Yrin, hear him voicing his doubts about the mission. I see Azari and the riot outside the glass temple. Most of all I re-run the hunt for Arden Xavier. That's right, tomorrow I play the game for real.

Seven

I wake early, eat breakfast early, but leave the hotel exactly on time. Sleep I couldn't. Act I must. The mission is planned down to the nanosecond. The intelligence says that Arden Xavier will wait until the last minute to make his move. I have to be close to President Shavlotan, in full view of the podium. From my vantage point I will be able to intercept Xavier. Security won't pick up my weapon. I will spot my quarry by his deformed antenna. Then I take him out. It's got to be a flesh wound. That way the interrogators can get the information to behead the Cerberus conspiracy. Simple. Only it isn't.

What about what Yrin Gok told me? This Arden Xavier, he has many faces. To some he is a Hoopwot, to others a human, to others a Meener. But I have a positive ID. He is a Threnassic. I will know him by the melted antenna. I hear the voices of Liesl Schlachthof and Yrin Gok battling in my head. So who do I trust? As I join the crowds making their way to the

Great Hall where the Peace Conference will take place I try to be single minded. I have to shut out Gok's voice, eliminate the doubts. Liesl recruited me. If she doesn't understand the mission, who the hell does? I reach Independence Square, the vast open space in front of the Presidential Palace. Shavlotan has just won his second five-year term of office. Once his inauguration for his new term is over, he will open the Peace Conference. I find myself frowning. It isn't like the game. It's broad daylight. When I tracked Arden Xavier in the game it was a moonless night. That's why I had to use the Night Bloom. Surely the rehearsal should have got a detail like the time of day right. The whole thing is unravelling.

The crowd is pressing forward. I feel the weight of the ZX90 in my backpack. I know it is going to slip through unnoticed, but somehow I have a nagging doubt. What if the police stop me? What if I'm caught in possession of a deadly weapon? How do I explain that I am there to stop an assassin, not to be one? Then I hear Liesl's reassuring voice. *The ZX90 is made of Metakyprosium, an element found only on Metakal in the Lycan-Thyperidean asteroid belt.* There is nothing to worry about. I am here to do good. Everything has been leading up to this moment. The game trained me for this, to stop Arden Xavier, to sever the first head of Cerberus and break the conspiracy.

So do it, Henry Kwok. Save the President. Be a hero. I am approaching the security cordon. It consists of a vast curving perimeter. Huge, steel obelisks stand at fifty-metre intervals. Silver light pulsates between them. It is designed to locate any hidden weapons, even the tiniest components. I take a deep breath and stride forward, confident that it won't pick up the ZX90. There are three cordons like this. The security police aren't taking any risks. Scores of heavily armed Threnassic officers weave their way through the crowd. They wave the spectators forward. I step into the fluorescent silver curtain. I'm through. I reach the second cordon. Through again.

I'm ready to breeze through the final band of light, but this time there is no easy passage. The instant I enter the cordon all hell lets loose. Alarms bray across the square. Security police converge on the area. They train their weapons on me. There is the menacing whine of power packs. One twitchy finger and I'm a stain on the ground.

"Put the bag on the floor, biped. *Put the bag on the floor!*"

My heart hammers.

"Do it!"

The crowd is melting away. Startled eyes fix me. Hardly able to breathe, I shrug off the backpack.

"Step back from the bag!"

I do as I'm told. Instantly, a pair of Threnassics throw me to the floor. I force my head up and watch with horror when they open the backpack and examine the weapon. As they drag me away, outraged citizens in the crowd rain down blows, making my ears ring. This is no re-run of the scenes from the game. I'm not a hero. I'm an.......

"Assassin."

"Traitor!"

Accusations whipcrack around me. Then there is a new cry, more menacing than all the others.

"Hand him over. We know what to do with him."

Things are getting ugly. The crowd is closing in, struggling with the security police. They're determined to get to me. They want to rip me to shreds. Hundreds, maybe thousands of onlookers are baying for my blood. The cops are protecting me for now, but what if their necks are on the line? Are they going to withdraw and abandon me to the mob? What's going to happen to me? The evidence is damning. I have been caught in possession of a deadly weapon when I was just metres from the President. Terror is squeezing me like a vice. How could this happen? The detectors weren't supposed to pick up the ZX90. What went wrong?

"This way, biped," barks the Threnassic next to me. "If you want to live, move!"

I look at him with startled eyes.

"Fine. Stay here. Die if you want to. It doesn't bother me either way. You're nothing but a sub-apeling terrorist."

I scramble to my feet and let him guide me away. I am being bundled through the press of the crowd. Meeners are breathing fire. Hoopwots are slashing at me. Threnassics are flailing with their pincers. I've just become public enemy number one. Suddenly a chaotic situation spins out of control. There is a loud thud and a shock wave ripples through the crowd. Screams and howls of panic follow. A split second later there is a second deafening crack. All around me the spectators are losing their footing and sprawling on the ground. Orange smoke floats through the air. People are yelling and scrambling for cover. Nobody knows what's happening. That includes the cops who are guarding me. Suddenly my captors have let go of my arms. I seize the moment and struggle away through the mayhem, elbowing bodies out of the way. I spot the backpack and seize it. I might just need the gun if they come after me. Within moments I am hurdling fallen bodies, trying to make my escape.

I happen to glance back. A wall of security police has formed in front of the Presidential Palace. Their ranks are bristling with weapons. What just happened, I wonder. There is no way of knowing. I sure as hell don't want to stop and ask. I've got to put everything to the back of my mind and concentrate on saving my neck. Somebody spots me.

"The assassin! There!"

I glimpse a dozen, maybe more, of the onlookers fixing me with hostile stares.

"Get him!"

They start to move in my direction. I can only think of one thing to do. I drop the backpack, open it, assemble it in moments and brandish it in front of them.

"Back off or I fire."

"He's got a gun!"

Instantly, the crowd surges away from me, like an inverse whirlpool. There is renewed panic. I fire off a shot into the air and take advantage of the madness around me to make my escape. The security cops are reluctant to leave their positions protecting the palace. Their first concern is to protect President Shavlotan and the Peace Conference delegates. The sound of the ZX90 has made my pursuers think again. Within moments I am sprinting through empty streets. Everybody is in the square. Just a few hundred metres from the madness in front of the palace there is an eerie silence. I skid round a corner and stumble back against a wall, gasping for breath.

What do I do? What *can* I do? I am two hundred years in the future, on a planet who knows how far from Earth and quite soon every cop and mercenary in the galaxy is going to come after me.

I shove myself off the wall and jog down the nearest alley, trying to gather my thoughts. I find myself in a broad piazza. There are giant screens beaming coverage of events in front of the Presidential Palace. I dart glances in every direction. Do I have time to watch the broadcast? The coast seems clear. I stare at the flashing images, trying to make sense of what has just happened. The broadcaster is running the same piece of film over and over again. I am twitchy, anxious. Every time I see movement on the street or a skyflitter skims the rooftops I expect a loudspeaker to crackle across the city, drawing attention to my presence.

When I finally focus on the news coverage I feel a sense of shock. They're running film of what happened. President Shavlotan walks to the podium. Just as he is about to start his speech there is a loud roar. Cameras sweep the crowd. Then there's my face. I watch the images of the security cops bundling me to the ground and examining the contents of my backpack. Even as close-ups of my face are relayed across the galaxy there is another roar. An emerald-clad figure flashes before the president. It's just a blur, but I know immediately who it is. I see the clip out. The familiar form appears. In the same split second there are two shots from a pulse weapon. One takes a chunk out of the wall behind President Shavlotan. The second tears a hole out of the paved area in front of the dignitaries. I am more confused than ever. That flashing, green form, it was Azari Azaal.

There is no time to dwell on the puzzle. A police skyflitter has dropped to street level and is gliding down the block no more than two metres off the ground. I start to back away. Wrong move. A laser cannon swivels. Sensors have picked up movement. Now the gunner is homing in on me. I start to run. A needle thin beam of light blows out a window. I run through the spray of glass fragments. One stings my skin. Damn, that hurt. I am pounding up an escalator. Simultaneously, the skyflitter rises. A shadow sweeps over me. Make that two skyflitters. Two more beams of light cross in the air. One misses me by centimetres. I spin round a corner and fire the ZX90. The skyflitters retreat momentarily then come after me again. I'm in trouble. Big trouble.

I am half running, half tumbling down the next escalator when a command echoes from the nearest skyflitter's speakers.

"Halt! Lay down your weapon. There is no escape. Give yourself up or we will use lethal force."

I'm wondering what just blew out the window if it wasn't lethal force. Tell me, what was that, gentle persuasion? I lose my footing and sprawl on the ground. I glimpse the approaching skyflitters out of the corner of my eye and scramble to my feet. I need my feet to move faster, but they're barely responding. My legs are like lead. One skyflitter is directly overhead. Security cops are starting to abseil, heavily armed Threnassics the lot of them. The other skyflitter is gliding behind me to block my escape. What do I do? The game didn't prepare me for this. The cops hit the streets.

"Lay down the weapon!" the nearest officer commands.

A dozen laser sights play across my chest and face. I swallow hard.

Eight

These guys are getting repetitive. I've got the ZX90 in my hands. I don't want to kill. Suddenly I know what I have to do. The Night Bloom feature can turn night into day. So what will it do when it's already light? I shut my eyes and twist the grip. The cops start to yell in agony, pincers clawing at their bug-eyed faces. They're blinded. OK, it will only be for a few moments, but the Night Bloom has done the trick. From somewhere I summon the strength to run. In the square I got scared. In the last few minutes I just got angry. I'm going to find out what's going on.

I am in the city's mean streets. The street lights are darker, the tenements bleaker, the different tribes of alien drifters more suspicious of me. Come to think of it, I am more suspicious of them. I feel about as safe as an egg in a tumble drier. That's the downside. The upside is the cops don't feel much safer. This is the kind of place where the cops go in mob-handed or they don't go in at all. They have a nasty habit of winding up dead.

The skyflitters are keeping their distance, but they haven't gone away. They're patient. They're locked on to my movements and they're waiting for an opportunity to pounce. The throbbing engines pound in my head. Right now they must be downloading my bio-rhythms into their database. I permit myself a quiet smile. Hard luck, guys. You're going to draw a blank. The kid from the past isn't going to show up. In this time and this place I'm a non-person. No sooner have I allowed myself that comforting thought than it comes back to haunt me.

"Henry Kwok," the speakers boom across the ghetto, "give yourself up." Fright scurries down my spine. That's impossible! How can they possibly have my bio-rhythms? How can they have any kind of record I even exist? I'm from two centuries in the past and half a universe away. Events had already turned crazy. Now they've just got crazier still.

"Henry Kwok," the speakers repeat, "give yourself up." Then an add-on that turns my blood to ice. "There is a reward of one hundred thousand credits for anyone who can capture Henry Kwok."

A searchlight sprays an image of my face across the sky. That's all I need, a call for the scum of Thren 15 to go on a Kwok hunt. Suddenly I'm a marked man. More skyflitters home in on me. They darken the sky. The good citizens of the ghetto come out and stare. I shrink back into a doorway. Any minute now mobs of the citizenry will be roving the streets, inspired by thoughts of what they could do with one hundred thousand credits. The speakers crackle again.

"We want the assassin Kwok dead or alive. Reward will be paid upon positive recognition."

Even as the voice fades I notice movement up ahead. A crowd of Hoopwots has descended on a passing humanoid. I see one of the leaders grab him by the hair and examine his features.

"This ain't no humanoid biped, you dumb skrit," he grumbles. "This here's a one-eyed apeling. He don't look a bit like that humanoid they just flashed up."

Thank goodness for dumb skrits who can't tell the difference between a one-eyed apeling and a very lonely and very scared Henry Kwok. I am still looking for somewhere to go when a hand closes over my face. I try to scream, but the grip is too powerful. The attacker drags me down an alley. I want to yell for help, but what good would that do? It would attract the cops or the roaming gangs of vigilantes or worse. Instead I claw at the hand that is gripping my face.

"Will you knock it off, young Kwok!" barks a familiar voice.

He removes his hand.

"Yrin!"

"I've been trying to catch up with you since you fled from the square. You may be new to Thren 15, but you're good. If it wasn't for the skyflitters I would have lost you."

"You've been following me?"

"Correct. This whole mission had me spooked. I was only meant to meet you on arrival. That was it, meet, greet and go. Forget you ever existed. I could have followed the brief and gone back to a life of anonymity."

"But you decided to shadow me?"

"You know what, kid?" Yrin says. "I decided you were being set up. Azari came to the same conclusion."

"I saw her outside the palace," I say.

"Of course you did," Yrin replies. "It was her actions that saved the president's life."

"That's what she was doing!"

Yrin has his eyes on the roaming gangs prowling the street. "As soon as I decided this whole thing was about as sweet as a Meener's poop, I went to see Ms Azaal and suggested we cooperate. I couldn't think of anyone else to trust."

He starts to doze off. I snap my fingers under his nose and he continues his story.

"I got to keep an eye on you. Azari got the job of seeing the Pres came to no harm. Looks like things worked out pretty well." He shrugs his shoulders. "Except..."

"Except?"

"Except all three of us are now on the run. Cerberus is on our tail. The cops are after us." He gives the vigilantes a meaningful glance. "Them too. Time to move, young Kwok."

"But there's nowhere to go," I protest.

"There's always somewhere to go."

"I don't get it."

"We can't go left or right," Yrin confirms with a grin. "We can't go up." He's right. The skyflitters are still hovering. "But we can go down."

He punches a code into a panel on the pavement and kicks back a manhole cover. I stare down the shiny, metallic shaft into the gloom below.

"The sewers? You've got to be kidding. What's down there?"

I see Yrin give a broad grin.

"Besides the obvious."

Yrin shrugs.

"You mean you don't even know what we're going to be jumping into?"

"Not a clue," he chuckles.

"That's mad."

Yrin winks. "Madness is my middle name. What's life without an element of chance? Are you ready?"

I'm still hesitating when the Hoopwots register our presence.

"There he is, over there with that Somnolent."

"Might have guessed they'd be working together."

"Yeah, bipeds and pillow-biters. Get them."

Yrin pinches his nose and jumps into the drain. I give a despairing groan and copy him. I've been falling for a few seconds when I hear Yrin's fall come to the end with a loud splash then a snort of disgust.

"Slopgrot!"

I hit the water a split second later. Only it isn't water. It's the foulest-smelling gloop it's ever been my experience to fall into.

"What *is* this stuff?" I groan.

"Did you not hear me call it Slopgrot?" Yrin demands.

"But what is it?" I ask, before thinking better of it. "No, I've changed my mind. Don't tell me."

Yrin nods. "Good call." He peers into the gloom. "Hold on to my shoulders."

I do as he says. Soon he is swimming powerfully down a pitch-black drain. There is no light.

"How do you know where you're going?"

"I don't. Somnolent warriors work on instinct. Everybody knows that. Where have you been hanging out?"

"A planet half a universe away and two centuries in the past."

Yrin give a grunt. "That would explain it."

He swims strongly and easily. I have little sensation of movement. After a few minutes I spot a pinprick of light.

"What's that?"

"Our destination."

"Where do we come out?"

"Not a clue."

"What!"

"I see a light and I go for it. We'll deal with the consequences when we arrive."

If Yrin has a philosophy of life it must be Que Sera Sera, what will be, will be. I strain to see what that is up ahead.

"Is that a waterfall?" I ask.

Yrin shrugs and almost pitches me into the slime.

"Sorry," he grunts.

"And what's that smell?" I ask.

"Will you stop asking questions?" Yrin growls. "I'm no expert on sewers. I've never been in one before."

The light that is streaming towards us is so strong it makes me blink. Even though I can't make sense of the shiny blur I am starting to feel uneasy. What *is* that smell?

"Yrin, swim slower."

"Why?"

"Just do it," I tell him. "That smell, I recognise it."

Then I have it.

"It's acid!"

"What?"

"You heard me. It's some kind of acid. They must use it to dissolve the Slopgrot."

Suddenly Yrin is trying to swim against the current. We are spinning in the surging tide. But the current is too strong. Any moment we are going to be swept into the acid waterfall.

Nine

I've seen Yrin puzzled. I've seen him concerned. I've never seen him scared. Not until now. We're both kicking, flailing, desperately trying to swim against the current, but it is too strong. It sweeps us forward, the immense power of the torrent carrying us like corks. No matter what we do, it is propelling us ever closer to the acid waterfall. Yrin's gaze drifts upwards. I notice a grim determination enter his eyes.

"What have you seen?"

"I'll keep swimming. You get that whip out of the holster."

"Whip? What are you, Indiana Jones?"

Not for the first time I glimpse incomprehension in his stare. There's no time to explain. While he struggles against the tide, I yank the whip from the leather holster. It is longer than a whip back home and it is made of metal links.

"What is this? It's not like any whip I've ever seen."

Yrin isn't talking. He swims with one arm and thumbs a switch with his free hand. It buzzes and the whip extends, racing up to a girder high above our heads. It wraps itself around the girder. Yrin presses the switch again and the whole thing stiffens. He flicks it again and we start to rise out of the gloop.

"Hold on tight!"

I cling to his belt. We are hurtling upwards at breathtaking speed. The trigger-mechanism gobbles up the metal links until we are dangling just below the girder. Yrin wraps an arm round it and pulls me up. We hang there, panting.

"Now what?" I ask.

Yrin nods in the direction of a manhole.

"We came down here through one of those. Time to climb out and see where we are."

We make it out of the manhole. I only have to wake him up once.

"This way," he tells me.

"So you know where we're going?"

"No."

"But...Oh, I get it, instinct."

"You're learning."

I see the pedestrians around us wrinkling their noses and nudging each other. At least nobody is going to approach a Somnolent and a humanoid biped dripping with thick, rancid Slopgrot. We reach a street corner. Yrin stops. His wristband is flashing. He whispers into it.

"Azari?"

She must have asked his location because he consults the tiny screen on the wristband.

"We're in District 21. What's that? Damn! OK, see you at the rendezvous."

"Something wrong?"

"Cerberus goons have bombed her breakfast bar. Looks like all three of us are on the run. The cops are after us. Cerberus is after us. Every vigilante and amateur manhunter in the city is after us. Odds against survival? Pretty much nil, I'd say."

This cracks me up.

"So why are we running?"

"Because fighting back is the right thing to do," Yrin answers. "For years now, I've allowed Cerberus to control me. They watch my every movement. Well, I'm not running scared any more. This time I..."

He starts to doze and I shake him awake.

"This time I fight back."

Somehow his rousing speech doesn't fill me with a great deal of confidence, especially when he nods off in the middle of it. It's three of us against the rest and what a trio: a fourteen-year-old kid, an eyeless Ninja woman and a warrior who falls asleep in the middle of a fight.

"We've got a few minutes' respite," Yrin drawls. "Let's use it well. We need to wash off this Slopgrot."

Not for the first time, the prediction that we have lost our pursuers turns to ash in his mouth. There is a power flash and a burst of lethal energy blasts a hole in the wall just centimetres from Yrin's head. We dive for cover. A second blast turns a passing apeling to dust. Wrong place. Wrong time.

"Cops?"

Yrin shakes his head.

"Cerberus. Lone assassin."

"How do they know where we are?"

Yrin frowns.

"Beats me. I thought we'd lost them for sure."

He draws a firearm and blasts away at the sniper. Within seconds the air is filling with skyflitters. Speakers bray commands.

"Clear the streets. Repeat. Clear the streets. The city is in lock-down. Anyone defying this order is in contravention of Public Order Law Nine. We will shoot on sight."

Panicky citizens run for their lives. They know this is no idle threat. Yrin takes my hand.

"It's been good knowing you, kid. Looks like our friendship ends here."

"You're kidding!" I yell. "You're giving up?"

"Oh, believe me, survival is my top priority, but we have to be realistic. I don't see either of us coming out of this alive."

"But we're going to try?"

He grins.

"Hell yes."

With that, we start to run. He offers me a weapon. I arm myself with the ZX90 and shake my head.

"I'll stick with this."

He nods. The skyflitters rain down fire. We shoot back with the reckless defiance of a couple of guys who think they're dead men walking. That's when we see the bus. It's a public transport skyflitter, abandoned when the driver ran for cover.

"Cover me," Yrin barks. "It will take me a few seconds to start the power drive."

While he fires up the engine, I pump shots at the cops.

"Henry Kwok, Yrin Gok, give yourselves up. Resistance is futile."

Yrin is ready.

"Get in," he yells.

We roar into the air pursued by half a dozen police skyflitters.

"Can we outrun them?" I ask.

"I doubt it."

"So what's the plan?"

No answer. He has just dozed off. He slips off the control panel and sprawls on the floor. I grab the controls. Within seconds I am weaving through heavy fire from the pursuing skyflitters.

"Yrin," I plead, jabbing at him with my shoe. "Yrin, wake up."

But he is snoring away. I give his foot a kick.

"What? What's wrong....? Oh, right."

He takes the controls.

"Do you think we can get through that space?" he asks.

I see the gap between two huge skyscrapers.

"No way. Yrin, you're crazy. Yrinnnnnnn!"

I'm still screaming when he squeezes between the buildings. The bus's wings clip the structures on either side but we make it. It buys us a few moments, but the police are still on our tail. There's a loud explosion and smoke fills the vehicle.

"We're hit," Yrin says.

He slaps a palm on a panel to his right. Equipment tumbles from the storage unit. He rummages through the mess and tosses me a backpack.

"Put it on."

"What is it?"

"Escape pack."

"Come again?"

"It's got enough propulsive power to get you to the ground."

"You're kidding! We're going to bail out?"

He nods at the dense smoke that is starting to fill the cabin.

"Got another idea?"

He clips on his own pack and punches a red button. Air rushes in.

"I can't," I protest.

Yrin grabs me by the arm and launches me out of the door.

"Count to five and hit the start button. Use the straps to steer."

His voice vanishes into the rush of wind. I count. I hit the start button. I grip the straps and try to control my progress. Already the ocean of skyscrapers is rushing towards me. I master this contraption or I'm an ex-Kwok. The controls are simple. Tug left and you veer left. Tug right and you veer right. I try to climb, but that isn't what the pack does. It slows your descent. That's all. So I glide earthwards, yanking on the straps to find somewhere to land. I'm trying to locate somewhere soft when I glimpse Yrin hurtling towards me. He is nodding ferociously to indicate something. There is a spacecraft standing on the banks of a glittering lake. I recognise the woman standing beside it.

It's Azari Azaal.

Ten

When I hit the ground it feels as if I've taken a blow from a giant hammer. My senses swim. I struggle for breath.

"You OK?"

I focus on Yrin's concerned face.

"Yes." I suck in a mouthful of air. "Yes, I'm fine."

I get up and instantly crumple back to the ground. Yrin hauls me to my feet and waves a hand in front of my face.

"How many fingers?"

"Five."

"Fine," he says. "You'll live. We've got to go."

He bundles me through the door of the space ship. Azari is already starting the power drive.

"Buckle up!" she commands.

I've barely fastened my safety belt when the craft lurches into the sky, slamming me back against the seat. The flitters are already on our tail. Cannon fire is buffeting our ship.

"That was too close for comfort," Azari hisses.

"Can we outrun them?" I ask.

I put the same question when we were on the bus. This time there is a more reassuring answer.

"We already have," Azari answers.

She raises the panels and I stare in disbelief. We're in outer space.

"That's incredible."

"This is a good ship," she says. "It's easy to get away from a few lumbering skyflitters. The real test will come when they launch their deep space pursuit craft."

"Can we outrun *them*?"

There is doubt in her voice.

"I don't think so. We need a better plan."

"And do you have one?"

There is no reply. Next to me Yrin shifts in his seat.

"The boy's asked you a question, Azari."

"We can't outpace them," she answers.

"Then we're finished."

She waits a beat.

"There is something we can do."

She types a command into the on-board computer and a star chart flashes up.

"Oh no," Yrin says. "No way."

"They're already scrambling their pursuit craft," Azari says. "They will catch us in less than two hours."

"But the Razono Vozela, that's suicide."

Azari sticks to her guns. "Nobody knows for sure."

"What's the Razono Vozela?" I ask. "What are you two talking about?"

Yrin answers. "Azari is planning to take us through the Razono Vozela radiation belt."

"And that's bad?"

"It's the most intense concentration of cosmic rays in the starways," Yrin explains. "Numerous adventurers have tried to run it. Those who have returned have died of radiation sickness within weeks ."

"And the rest?"

Yrin shrugs. "Nobody knows. None of them was heard of again."

"So that's our options?" I ask, hope draining from my voice. "We stick to charted space and they destroy us or we enter this Razono Vozela thing and most likely we'll die of radiation sickness anyway?"

Yrin nods. "That's about the size of it."

Azari taps the control panel to get our attention. "I say we vote. I'm for entering the radiation belt. It's certain death if we stay in charted space."

I don't believe I'm saying it, but I wind up agreeing with her. "Let's do it. Yrin?"

He consults the computer. The flight projection shows Threnassic starships closing on us. "How long before they intercept us?"

"Less than an hour," Azari answers grimly.

"Can we reach Razono Vozela in time?"

Azari nods. "But we have to change course now."

Yrin gives in. "Then I don't see we've got much choice."

Azari changes course. As we enter the radiation belt the pursuing starships peel away. Their commanders must think we're crazy.

"They're giving us up for dead," Azari says.

I venture a question.

"Do you think they're right?"

Azari shrugs. "We'll just have to wait and see."

The scene outside doesn't look any different, but at that very moment cosmic rays could be killing us. It seems strange, just sitting there wondering if some unseen force is eating away at your bones, your flesh, your vital organs. I always thought I would scream and fight and cry and protest and fight for my life. Now here I am, facing the greatest danger in my whole existence and I am just taking it, accepting that an invisible enemy could be eating me from the inside out. I decide to break the gloomy silence.

"Something I don't get," I say, turning to Azari. "You jumped in the way of the president. Does that mean you saw Arden Xavier."

"Oh, I saw her all right."

I find myself staring at her.

"Run that by me again," I say. "Did you just say *her*?"

"That's right. The assassin was a female. I kicked the weapon from her hands. She fled into the crowd. Unfortunately, that's not the way President Shavlotan's people see it. They've got a weapon and a blurred image of me. Put the two together and Azari Azaal is top of the most wanted list."

An idea, barely formed, is working its way from the back of my mind.

"This female assassin, what did she look like?"

"She was a humanoid biped like you."

The idea is taking shape.

"What colour hair did she have?"

Azari frowns. "Do you know something?"

"I might do. So? Was she blonde, brunette, redhead?"

"She was blonde."

Now the idea is like lava spewing from a volcano.

"Do you think the cameras caught her?"

"I don't know. Her image must be somewhere in the footage. Why?"

"Somebody sent me here. My information was that the assassin was a Threnassic, some eight-limbed bug-boy called Arden Xavier." I glance at Yrin. "Then you go and tell me nobody really knows what our master criminal looks like. Seems Cerberus has been spreading false trails all over the galaxy. Everybody has their own Arden Xavier."

Yrin is on my wavelength. "So you want to look at the footage?"

"Got a better idea?" I ask. "It beats dwelling on the effect the Razono Vozela radiation belt is having on us."

Yrin taps a search into the computer. I have to nudge him awake twice. Finally, he gets the job done. After maybe two minutes there is an eight-way split-screen. I tap the first panel. There's a blur of golden hair. I tap the second. Still nothing conclusive. We have reached the seventh when I notice something.

"Can we enhance this detail in the corner?"

"Yrin taps in an instruction."

"What's that?"

Yrin examines the screen. "It's somebody's arm. The material looks like leather."

I close my eyes. You idiot, Henry Kwok. It's been staring you in the face all this time and you didn't realise.

"Something wrong?"

"I know why Cerberus is always one step ahead," I groan. "I know how the cops got my bio-rhythms. I know why the ZX90 set off the sensors." I take a breath. "I know the identity of Arden Xavier."

Yrin and Azari are hanging on my every word.

I tap the eighth panel of the split-screen. There she is, long, golden blonde hair, stunning azure eyes, black and scarlet motorcycle leathers. "Meet Arden Xavier aka Liesl Schlachthof."

Story two: the second head of Cerberus.

One

"She's played me for a patsy," I groan. "I'm a sucker, a fall guy."

I remember how I went all cow-eyed over the delicious Ms Schlachthof, hanging on her every word, believing every lie she spun. She only had to flutter her eyelashes and I swallowed every word she said. I was so gullible, a stupid kid who got over-excited about dreams of being a hero. I was playing a game and all the time she was making up the rules.

"I've been used."

Azari agrees. "This whole thing has been a set-up from start to finish. Xavier or Schlachthof or whatever her real name is has been acting on behalf of Cerberus all the time. She needed a diversion. It couldn't be somebody from our time. They wouldn't even have got into the square."

"Bio-rhythms records."

"Precisely."

"But I got through the first two cordons."

"Of course you did," Azari says. "Think about it, Henry. They wanted you to. They needed you as close to the Pres as possible. That way you diverted attention from their assassination attempt. My guess is they waited until you were through the second cordon then they downloaded the composition of the ZX90 and your bio-rhythms into their database. They get you right where they want you. Then bam, it's alarm time. Oh, they're clever."

"More than clever," Yrin grunts. "This whole conspiracy is the work of an evil genius."

"Are you trying to make me feel better?" I ask. "At least I haven't been suckered by an idiot?"

"No," Azari says grimly. "We are all as clever or as stupid as each other. We've all been deceived by a very impressive intelligence. She scoops

71

some kid out of another place and another time. He's clever. He's physically fit. There is enough in their choice of fall guy to be just about plausible to...."

I hear the catch in her voice. She doesn't finish.

"What were you going to say, Azari?"

"It doesn't matter."

"Oh, it matters. Say it."

"It's plausible to somebody impressionable. It's not a criticism, Henry. You're an adolescent boy. You wanted an adventure. She provided it."

Yrin picks up the train of thought. "Don't feel bad, Henry. We haven't done any better than you did. Cerberus picks out a couple of loners on the margins of society. Azari belongs to a group of people demonised as terrorists. They give her a chance to make amends for past mistakes. She is one of your contacts. The other is me, a guy from the most pathetic bunch of losers in the galaxy, a race of great warriors that fall asleep in the heat of battle."

"So all this was designed so that they could kill President Shavlotan and topple his government?"

"Exactly. Then Cerberus and the Expansion Alliance pick up the pieces and take power."

Yrin wanders over to the star chart. I watch him staring at our position. "What are you thinking, Yrin?"

"I'm thinking I would love to...."

He slumps forward, snoring into the screen. I go over and shake him awake.

"I'm thinking," he continues, "we should go back and prove Cerberus wrong. They chose us because we're outsiders, losers." He clenches his fist. "I say we go back and show them losers can be winners."

I turn and look at Azari. "I'm in. What about you?"

She gives a slight nod. "Let's do it."

But we don't do it. Suddenly we can't do anything. An ominous shape has appeared on our scanners.

"What's that?"

Yrin stares. "I have no idea." He rushes for the controls and disengages autopilot. "It's big."

"Can we take evasive action?" Azari asks.

"Exactly what I'm trying to do."

There is panic in her voice.

"It's closing!" I cry, watching an object at least twenty times bigger than our craft looming ever closer.

"We've got a visual," Yrin announces.

I turn and stare at the approaching vessel. Huge metal jaws yawn open. It's trying to swallow us.

"Can we outrun it?"

"No chance," Yrin answers.

"It's like that James Bond movie," I gasp before realising neither the words *James Bond* nor the word *movie* will mean anything to my companions. The great maw of the vessel swallows us. I stare up at the colossal structure, the lights, the girders, the engines. The jaws pass us then start to close. In a matter of minutes they clamp shut.

We're trapped.

We sit there for over an hour. From time to time machinery hums and clanks, but it is always a false start. Eventually something happens. Giant, steel clamps grip the fuselage of our spacecraft. Yrin kills the engines.

"Looks like we're going to meet our captors any moment now."

Azari makes her way to the passenger doors and listens. "They've got drilling equipment. Is there any point resisting?"

"What are you saying?" I ask. "We just let them in?"

"If there is any chance of getting out of here," Azari answers, "we will need this ship. If they drill their way through that door, it will be unusable." She drums her fingers. "Well, do you want to be here forever? I need an answer."

Yrin thinks for a moment then nods. "She's right. If they damage that door we've got no way home."

"Fine," I concede. "Let them in."

Azari hits a panel and the door hisses open. It is a few moments before we get a first glimpse of our captors.

"Stand clear!" comes a command.

The first member of the boarding party thuds down the steel ladder. He is wearing a black, protective suit and helmet. He turns and raises his visor. In spite of myself, I let out a gasp of horror. One side of his face is a molten mass of burned flesh and tatters of loose skin. The destruction wrought to his face has obliterated his right eye socket entirely.

"Does my face repel you, humanoid?" he snarls.

When I fail to answer, he roars a command.

"Answer me!"

"No...I mean, what happened to you?"

He gives a lopsided grin. "Most of our captives are too terrified to speak. It's like this, humanoid. The Razono Vozela radiation belt happened to me. That's right, look upon my ruined features. This is what lies in store for you if you stay here."

More members of the boarding party filter into the cabin. One after another, they lift the visors. Each time it is the same story. Withered flesh, missing ears, noses and eyes, tattered, hanging skin. The Razono Vozela has made them monsters.

"We are the Kur Zhen," the leader announces. "We serve the Jumeli, ruler of this realm. I am Zul, commander of the palace guard."

He approaches me.

"Good, good," he says. "You are young."

I wonder why that's good. Something tells me I won't like the answer. I don't think they're planning to open a school out here. He pulls a device from his belt and points it at me. A silvery light plays over me.

"No congenital illnesses. No genetic defects. Excellent."

He moves on to Yrin and repeats the operation with the scanner.

"You have a sleeping disorder."

Yrin folds his arms. "I am a Somnolent. It is my condition."

Zul snaps his fingers. "Take this one to a holding cell. He will do for parts."

"Parts! You will not dismember me. I can crush you to dust with my fists." Yrin struggles for a moment. "I can smash your skull with...." Then he dozes off in mid sentence. Zul shakes his head.

"Somnolents."

He turns and marches over to Azari.

"Remove the veil."

Azari lifts her veil as ordered. The Kur-Zhen see her eyeless face and murmur in dismay.

"You are not new to the Razono Vozela, I see."

Azari senses an opportunity. They don't know about the Azaals' condition. "No."

"She is tainted," Zul observes. "Interview her. See what skills she has and put her to work. Keep her under supervision." He jabs my chest with a gloved finger. "This one goes to the Jumeli. He is perfect."

The Kur Zhen guards drag me up the ladder onto the roof of the ship and march me across one of the walkways attached to the fuselage. The dimensions of the craft that has swallowed our ship are mind-boggling. I allow my gaze to wonder around the walls. It takes some time before I realise what I am staring at. There are vast hoards of precious metals.

"That's right," the guard nearest me says. "The Jumeli has vast wealth. Many are the pirate crews that would love to raid us, but they dare not cross the Razono Vozela."

I am still staring with bewilderment at the vastness of the interior when the guards shove me roughly through a door. Where the ship was stark and gloomy, this area is luxurious. There are tapestries and wall hangings, fountains and plants. The furniture is beautifully designed and made of all kinds of materials, many of which are unlike anything on Earth. Soon Zul arrives.

"Kneel," he barks.

"What?"

"Kneel, humanoid. Avert your eyes until you are told otherwise. The Jumeli is about to enter."

He kicks the back of my legs and I kneel, bowing my head. I hear footsteps. The Kur Zhen click the heels of their military boots.

"You may raise your head," Zul tells me.

When I look up, my jaw drops.

Two

Picture this.

Standing in front of me is a creature constructed out of two separate parts, one male, one female. The male section is a three-metre tall icicle creature. The female section is a mirror image of her brother and she is squatting in the middle of his rib cage watching me with intense, crystal eyes. I am still recovering from my surprise at seeing this curious hybrid of lifeform and icicle when her voice crackles through the air.

"This one may do," she hisses. "We feel his warmth from here."

As the final word escapes her frosted lips she leaps down from her perch in her brother's stomach and scampers across the floor to examine me up close. I can feel the intense cold emanating from her body. Already there are glittering, icy gems scattered across my skin. She pokes me with a frozen finger and a sheen of frost spreads across my flesh. I flinch at the sharp sting of her fingertip. She withdraws her hand and chuckles.

"Does my touch chill you?"

"It's painful."

She pokes me again and I start in pain.

"Stop it!"

She tosses back her head and shrieks with laughter. Then her eyes flash.

"Did you see our jewels and trinkets?"

"Yes."

"I bet you would like to get your hands on our hoard."

"No, honestly."

She screams with laughter.

"Honestly? Do you know how rare an honest citizen is in this galaxy?" She glances at the male part. "We should have him, brother."

Have him. I don't like the sound of that. Have him? As in for dinner...? She sprints back to her perch in her twin's stomach.

"Well, what do we think?"

"We are in agreement. His energy is...appetising."

To make things worse, I feel very alone without Yrin and Azari. I hope they are all right. I find the way the Jumeli is staring at me unsettling. Or should that be the way the Jumeli *are* staring? The voracious looks continue to wander over me, causing me even more discomfort. Maybe it is the glacial stares. Maybe it is the hunger that glitters from its, I mean their silvery pupils. Either way, I know this can't be good. The female part snaps her fingers.

"Prepare him, Zul."

They're going to prepare me. It sounds painful. It sounds, well, terminal.

"Move humanoid," Zul snarls.

"There's no need to push," I protest.

"You really think you're something, don't you?"

Zul shoves me again. Why does he hate me so much? Then I see the resentful stare and I understand. I remind him what it must feel like to be healthy, whole. I remind him of the way he was before the Razono Vozela did its worst. Now he is rotting.

"Is it painful?" I ask, looking at his tattered flesh.

Zul strikes me across the face so hard I crumple to the floor. He kneels next to me and hisses in my ear.

"Of course it is painful, you fool. Can you imagine what it feels like to have your body disintegrate before your very eyes?"

I struggle to my feet, wiping the blood from my nose.

"No."

"That's right, you can't. Nobody can."

"I'm sorry."

"Don't pity me," Zul snorts. "My agony is nothing compared to the horrors you will suffer when the Jumeli begins extraction."

"Extraction?"

"The Jumeli would suffer the fate of the Kur Zhen if it were not for the extractions."

"What happens when you're....extracted?"

Zul pushes me forward. He wants the thought of extraction to torture me.

"Keep walking," he orders.

I do as he says.

"Will you tell me what happens?"

He shrugs.

"You may as well know what we are going to do to you. The Jumeli survives by cryonic stasis. The Jumeli lives in a partially frozen state to arrest the progress of radiation sickness. When some unwitting traveller comes the Jumeli's way extraction follows."

"But what is it?"

"The Jumeli wants your warmth. For a few hours the Jumeli will be complete. The Jumeli will be happy."

"What about me? What happens to *me*?"

Zul marches me down a long corridor and slams me against a window. "See for yourself, humanoid."

I look upon a gruesome scene. A score of emaciated bodies float in jets of freezing gas. For a moment I think they are corpses then one of them, a girl, becomes aware of me watching. Her eyes open. I see her mouth move. It isn't difficult to read her lips. Her plea chills me. I know what she is saying.

Let me die.

"Is that how the Jumeli stays alive?" I ask.

"That's how the Jumeli does it. Each of these wretched creatures is a battery. With every day that passes the Jumeli needs more and more extractions to prevent the living death I and my fellow Kur Zhen suffer."

Zul kicks the back of my legs and I stumble to a cell.

"Get in there," he orders.

I do as I'm told. As the door starts to slide shut Zul grins.

"When I return the extraction will begin."

I pace up and down. Pain, he said, terrible pain. I suppose these moments are for me to prepare myself. But how do you prepare for torture? How do you get yourself ready to turn into a lifeform battery? There are moments when I wonder if this isn't some kind of crazy nightmare. I mean, is it possible? Can I really have travelled two hundred years in time and half a universe to end up as some kind of living dead? Have I really been framed up for an assassination attempt and turned into a fugitive from justice? Can any of this be real? Maybe it is all part of the game. A voice will announce game over and I will be me again, Henry Kwok, living in a flat in Hong Kong overlooking a busy world city.

But the game does not end. I sit. I stand. I try to think of some way to overcome Zul and make my escape. But what can I do against a ruthless warrior who is twice as strong as I am? Presently I hear the sound of footsteps. Boots scrape on the floor outside my cell. I brace myself. This is it. My rollercoaster adventure has led to this, a living death. The door slides open. Zul is standing in the doorway. But there is something wrong. His stare is hard and fixed in the distance. Suddenly he drops to his knees before me and falls forward. I see the reason why.

"Yrin."

"The guards were no match for me. I crushed their skulls like seed pods. I...."

He has just dozed off. He starts to sway.

"Yrin!"

His eyes snap open.

"What? Wh...? Oh, that again." He glances left and right along the corridor. "Let's go."

"Azari?"

79

"We will collect her on the way."

"We're going to the ship?"

Yrin nods.

"Of course. That is the only way we can escape."

"But how do we get out of the hull of this vessel?"

Yrin shrugs.

"We will cross that bridge when we get to it."

"That's your plan?" I ask. "We make it up as we go along?"

Yrin runs his fingers through his crimson hair.

"Have you got a better idea?"

I think for a moment.

"No."

Three

We free Azari with little problem. Yrin was right. He can snap the average Kur Zhen in half with his fists. Just when our escape is looking too easy to be true we hear the emergency alarm wailing across the cavernous interior of the Jumeli's battleship.

"This way," Azari hisses.

"How do you know?"

"I pay attention to my surroundings. Follow me. There's somebody I want you to meet."

We follow her through a series of sliding doors to a loading bay.

"Troya," Azari whispers. "You can come out. I'm with friends."

Troya is a tiny, crooked figure, a female apeling with huge, pleading eyes. She looks like an adolescent gorilla, but her face is more human, more alert and intelligent than any primate I have seen.

"This is Troya Simianova. She was in the work unit they sent me to," Azari explains. "Tell them what you told me."

"You have one chance of survival," Troya says, urgency written in her face. "The Jumeli stays alive by using the bodies of captives as batteries.

If we can reverse the polarity, the Jumeli perishes."

"Reverse the polarity," I say. "A bit like crossing the streams."

Troya stares. "Is this one sub-intelligent?"

The Ghostbusters reference has fallen on deaf ears.

"The monster's victims return to life," Troya continues. "The Jumeli's own life forces will protect you as you cross the Razono Vozela."

"But how do we do it?" Yrin asks.

"I can help you with that," Troya answers. "Just take me with you. My imprisonment here has been a terrible thing. I long to return to my home forests on Thren 6." She closes her eyes and her nostrils flare. "If only I could inhale the scents of the thorn bushes one more time."

Yrin smiles. "It's a bargain. So what's the plan?"

I see Troya's big eyes staring at me. Oh no, what's my part in her plan? I've got a feeling I'm not going to like this.

"It depends on the humanoid," she says.

Time for me to protest. "I do have a name, you know!"

"Sorry," she mutters. "I have been around the Kur Zhen too long. I have started to adopt their manners. You must return to the Jumeli, Henry Kwok. When they begin the extraction, I will reverse the polarity."

"What if it goes wrong?"

Troya looks confused.

"What if it doesn't work?"

"No, I understood you the first time," she answers. "I thought that was obvious. You become a human battery. You endure a living death." She glances at my companions. "Is his IQ limited. Is that not clear?"

"Oh, it's clear!"

"Something I don't understand," says Yrin. "Even if we reverse the polarity, how does that ensure our escape?"

"There are enough living batteries to rise up against the Kur Zhen. Under your leadership, they can win a great victory."

"They've got no weapons."

"We have weapons," Troya explains. "We have established an underground in the warehouses and loading bays of this vast ship, preparing for the day when the Jumeli's slave workers could rise up. There are escaped slave workers hidden in the holds. Free our comrades and we will equip them with the arms we have stolen from the Kur Zhen."

"Let's do it," says Yrin after a quick doze.

"Now hang on a minute," I say. "I have two questions. One, am I supposed to give myself up?"

"I will return you to the Jumeli," Azari explains. "I will tell them I am turning you in to save my own neck. They are used to turncoats. They will believe my story. What is your second question?"

"How far does this extraction go before Troya can reverse the polarity?"

"Not far," says Troya.

Somehow that doesn't sound very reassuring.

"How far is *not far* exactly? Will it hurt?"

"A little."

We argue over the plan for a few minutes then Azari puts it into operation. She walks straight into the Kur Zhen barracks and offers to hand me over. It isn't long before a hatch slides open and Azari points me out to the Kur Zhen. I play my part well, acting the betrayed friend.

"How could you, Azari?" I cry as they drag me out struggling.

Azari looks away as if ashamed.

"You hand me over to the Jumeli?" I yell. "Are you insane? They will use me then they will kill you."

"You're wrong there," says Zul. "Your friend Azari will come in very useful. She has a ruthless, immoral streak we like."

I fight to get at Azari. Zul beats me to the ground and drives his boot into my ribs. I slump to the ground, gasping for breath.

"The extraction proceeds immediately," he barks. "I will enjoy watching you being turned into a living battery. And I will enjoy making that Somnolent suffer."

"You will have to find him first," I retort defiantly.

"Oh, we'll find him," Zul says, slapping me across the head. "He will wish he had never been born."

I rub my sore head. This defiance act is causing me a lot of pain. Ten minutes later I am lying on a slab in the great hall of the ship with all kinds of tubes crawling all over me. Zul looks down at me with a studied cruelty. He hates everybody with skin that doesn't fall off and he is going to enjoy seeing me suffer. I have this urge to rip the creep's face off, but that is pretty hard to do when you are flat on your back with tubes coming out of you. The Jumeli enters the room. I hear the creature before I see it...him...her...they.

"We are ready," the Jumeli says. "We have been feeling faint of late. This infusion of humanoid life force is going to revive us."

Somebody flips a switch and I feel my blood rushing. This is going to hurt. I know it's going to....aaaarrrgh! Suddenly I feel like somebody reached inside me and flipped me inside out. The pain is excruciating. I can hear somebody screaming. It is a few moments before I realise it's me.

"That's good, so good," the Jumeli says, throwing back both heads in a gesture of rapture.

I try to rip out the tubes, but Zul has got me tied down to the slab by a series of restraints. I am tossing from side to side, but nothing I do reduces the pain or helps me get free.

"Please!" I howl. "Make it stop."

Zul laughs in my face.

"What's wrong, battery boy?" he smirks. "Wishing you had never crossed the Razono Vozela?"

I manage a snarl of defiance. "I'm wishing I'd never seen your ugly mug."

At that very moment there is a scream from across the room and the blood drains from Zul's face.

"What is wrong, Majesty?" he asks.

The Jumeli is shrieking in pain. "We are in agony. What did you do?"

"I didn't...."

Zul vanishes out of sight. I can hear him tapping questions into the computer.

"No," he cries. "It's impossible."

"What is it?" the Jumeli demands. "What have you discovered?"

"Somebody has reversed the polarity," Zul reveals. "Your life force is flowing out."

"Then make it stop," the Jumeli begs. "We are dying."

"I can't," Zul says. "Once the process has begun, the only way to stop it is to find the operator."

"Then find the dog!" the Jumeli roars. "We can't stand this a moment longer."

I hear running footsteps as the Kur Zhen fan out to search the ship. Meanwhile, the pain has vanished. In fact, I have never felt this good in my entire life. I lie still, enjoying the warmth that is rippling through me. I know that simultaneously, all the living batteries in their jets of frozen gas are starting to come back to life. If everything works to plan there will soon be an army coming to our aid.

Four

Things don't go to plan. I am just lying here. There are no gunshots, no sounds of struggle. Where's Yrin? What's Azari doing? What's happening? All kinds of questions are flooding through my mind when the Jumeli looms into view above me. The male face is creased with pain. The female face is glowering with rage.

"Are you part of this?" the female part shrieks, frosty spittle peppering my face. She points to somebody across the room. "Is she?"

The Jumeli turns. Azari must be there, just out of sight.

"We will not let you destroy us, humanoid," the Jumeli roars, that soul-chilling voice mutating from male to female and back again. "All who stand against us are destroyed." The Jumeli's faces come closer. "First, we make our enemies suffer all the horrors of Hell."

Oh great. First extraction. Now the horrors of Hell.

"I didn't do anything," I protest feebly. "I don't know what you're talking about."

I hear thudding boots and the Jumeli turns to listen to a report. It's Zul.

"It's the apeling Troya, the one who escaped from Section 35. She is behind all this. Nobody else has that level of scientific knowledge."

"Are you telling me a stinking primate has done this?"

"She is no ordinary primate...."

"Can she stop our pain?"

"Yes."

"Then find her!" the Jumeli bawls. "We are hurting so badly." The female part hugs the male part's neck. "We must be strong. We must show no weakness." But the male part is wailing with self-pity. "We can't stand it. It is so bad!"

I stare at the amazing sight of this strange being quarrelling with itself. "It is all right for us to say, but we can feel our life force ebbing away."

The female part turns on me. "If you have anything to do with this, we will make you wish you had never been born. We drink vengeance like wine." The Jumeli jabs an icy finger at Azari. "That goes for you too."

Several minutes crawl by then Azari leans over.

"Stay strong," she whispers.

"But where's Yrin?"

"I don't know."

She retreats suddenly. The Jumeli must have seen her approach me.

"What are you doing there, Azaal?" the female part demands. "You know something."

"Torture the Azaal," the male part commands. "Make her talk."

Everything is going wrong. Where are you, Yrin? I can hear Azari struggling with the guards. Suddenly the air shudders above me and a loud explosion rips a hole in a roof girder. Dust and metal fragments shower me. Guards bark orders. Beams of light criss-cross in the air. I hear a grunt of surprise then Yrin appears. He has just started to free me from my restraints when he slumps over me, snoring loudly.

"Not now," I groan.

Azari shakes him awake and he finishes the job. I struggle to my feet. A full-scale firefight is underway. The Jumeli is stumbling towards the door. The female part is firing a pulse weapon. The male part is wailing piteously.

"We are fed up of our whining," the female part snaps.

"We've got to get away," the male part sobs.

"Our parents chose the wrong part to play host," the female part says, with a shake of the head. "Why did they have to assume the male part was stronger? Our masculinity is pathetic."

"Is it done?" I ask, gazing at Yrin. "This reverse polarity thing, has it been successful?"

"Troya thinks so," Yrin answers. "She says the process has been put in motion. Now it is just a matter of time."

That's the good news. The bad news is that the Kur Zhen have the upper hand in the battle in the great hall.

"We've got to retreat," Azari says. "They've got us outnumbered. Where are these living batteries Troya promised?"

"It's bad news," Yrin replies. "They have been in those gas jets for a long time. They are taking longer to revive than Troya expected."

I don't like what I'm hearing. "Can't she hurry them up?"

"Easier said than done," Yrin tells me, clubbing one of the Kur Zhen to the ground. "She's trying her best."

He fires a round into the advancing Kur Zhen and pushes me through the door. "Let's go."

I follow Yrin, Azari and the small group of fugitive slave workers along a series of walkways. All the while pulse rifles are thudding around us. Yrin crashes his fist into a panel and we tumble through a door. To our relief we are met on the other side by a welcome sight. Troya has finally revived the living batteries. When the first of the Kur Zhen burst through the door after me, a withering hail of fire meets them. Half a dozen lie dead on the floor. The rest execute a disorderly retreat.

"Secure the door!" Yrin barks.

I glance at Troya. "How long before this reverse polarity thing has done its job?"

"You will know soon enough," she says. "It starts with extreme itchiness all over your body."

I start scratching.

"Then you start sneezing."

"Atishoo."

"Then you feel very hot."

Sweat stains my clothing.

"OK, it's happening," I tell her. "Now what?"

"Now we go and see what's happening to the Jumeli."

Yrin and Azari lead the way back outside. To our surprise there is nobody there. We make our way back to the great hall. We don't meet any resistance. When we reach our destination we see the reason why. The Jumeli is lying in the middle of the floor. I stare at the icy body melting away. The twin heads are butting each other furiously as the process of disintegration accelerates.

"We are finished," the male part wails. "Oh, cruel world."

"We are ashamed of us," the female part retorts. "Don't let the enemy see us weak."

"We don't care what the enemy thinks of us," the male part blubbers. "We are so miserable."

Then the Jumeli is gone. There is nothing but a pool of liquid. Zul drops his weapon.

"The Kur Zhen surrender," he says. "There is nothing left to fight for."

Yrin kicks the weapon away.

"Disarm them," he orders. "Lock them in the cells. We will decide what to do with them later."

Five

We don't do anything with the Kur Zhen. They have a ship. They can go anywhere they want. It is their decision. Can they survive? Has the radiation sickness that has rotted their bodies gone too far for them to recover? Questions are easy. Answers are reluctant creatures. Troya carries out tests on all the living batteries, and that includes me. She prods. She probes. She scans.

"It's done the trick," she says. "The life force of the Jumeli will give you the protection you need to make it back through the Razono Vozela without any permanent harm."

I have a question.

"What about Yrin and Azari? What about the escaped slave workers?"

"Those of you who took part in the reversal of polarity can give them a transfusion," she answers.

"This Jumeli life force," I ask, "aren't we stretching it a bit thin?"

"There is an element of risk," Troya agrees. "Are you willing to take the gamble?"

I glance at my friends.

"Yes."

"Good," Troya says. "That is true of everyone here. Apeling or humanoid, Azaal or Somnolent, we are brothers and sisters under the skin."

Yrin glances at a grumpy looking giant spider everybody is calling the Arachnibrid. "Does that go for spider boy too?"

"It goes for all of us," Azari says.

Yrin grins. "Just asking. I have this thing about eight-legged people."

The Arachnibrid snorts. "Watch it, biped."

The transfusions take a matter of minutes. Soon everyone is crowding around the star charts.

"There is a decision to be made," Yrin tells the crowd. "You are all from all over the galaxy. You have a choice. The first course is obvious. You can return home."

Troya frowns. "And the second?"

"Cerberus is close to power. Its agents have tried to assassinate President Shavlotan once already. They are bound to try again. They are biding their time for the next attempt. I say we go back and..."

To my horror, I see that he has nodded off halfway through his attempt at an inspirational speech to rally the troops. I elbow him hard in the ribs. Yrin looks embarrassed, but he continues until the Arachnibrid interrupts.

"What kind of leader is he going to be? He can't even stay awake."

Yrin drops his head.

"As you can see, I suffer a terrible affliction. Like all Somnolents, I drift off at regular intervals."

Troya moves closer to him.

"I have heard of this condition," she says. "I find it hard to believe that it is the natural condition of your people."

"It isn't," Yrin answers. "Our tragedy began the night of the Great Aurora ten long years ago."

Troya frowns. "What Great Aurora is this?"

"The Great Aurora that occurred on our home planet of Magentigor."

"Yrin," Troya says thoughtfully, "I am a scientist and I know of no such phenomenon."

"It happened. All our people gathered on Independence Night to commemorate the founding of the Republic of Magentigor."

"What happened? Exactly."

Troya is staring at him with big, dark, intense eyes.

"Our people gathered."

"The Somnolents?"

"We were not called that then. We are the Magenti." He runs his fingers through his deep red mane. "We are so called because of our hair."

"So you became Somnolents that night...because of this Aurora?"

"Yes. Why?"

"Because, my friend, there was no natural aurora that night on the planet of Magentigor."

89

"You are wrong," Yrin protests. "I saw it with my own eyes. It was the beginning of our long agony."

"Listen to me carefully," Troya says slowly. "There was no *natural* aurora that night."

Yrin stares at her for maybe ninety seconds then his eyes widen. "Are you saying there was some intelligence behind this? Are you saying we were made this way by a conscious act of malice?"

Troya nods. "That is exactly what I am saying."

Yrin thinks for a moment then growls angrily. "Cerberus."

Troya is onto something. "President Shavlotan was making his name as a Senator about then," she says. "Am I right?"

Yrin nods.

"The Somnolents...I mean the Magenti supported him. He was the peace candidate."

"Of course. We were sick of war. We wanted peace. He was the man to deliver it."

"Then this was done to break your people, Yrin."

Yrin stumbles to a console and leans on it, head bowed. "How could we have been so stupid? We accepted it as an act of chance."

"There is some good news," Troya tells him. "Just as we were able to do something about the Jumeli, we can do something about this condition."

Yrin turns. "Is this true?"

"The aurora must have been some kind of ray designed to alter your genetic make-up. If we can find out what it was we can create an antidote."

"With the Magenti restored to their former power," Azari exclaimed, "we can break Cerberus for good."

Yrin nods. "What do I have to do?"

"Lie down over there," Troya answers. "I have to carry out some tests."

While she examines Yrin I sit with Azari.

"In this fight against Cerberus, do you think we can win?"

"That is the wrong question," Azari murmurs.

90

"So what is the correct question?"

"You ask whether what you are doing is right. You will find out whether doing the right thing is possible in the heat of battle."

I find myself nodding. "Yes, I like that. When did you get so wise?"

"I didn't get wise," Azari answers. "I got here."

"Sounds a bit like me," I sigh. "You know what, we think we make our own decisions, but it isn't true. Sometimes life is just a bunch of accidents."

Azari laughs. "When did *you* get so wise?"

I notice Yrin sitting up.

"Well," I ask, "what's the verdict, doc?"

Troya examines me with her huge eyes. "We can create a laser treatment to correct the Somnolents' condition."

"That's great."

"The next bit isn't so great," Yrin says. "There is only one source for the material she wants to use as an antidote."

"And what's that?"

"We need Metakyprosium," Troya says. "lots of it and Metakyprosium is an element found only on..."

I finish her sentence. "Metakal, in the Lycan-Thyperidean asteroid belt."

Troya blinks. "How did you know that?"

"My gun," I explain. "The ZX90 is made of the same stuff." I frown. "I wonder what the Kur Zhen did with it."

The Arachnibrid grunts. "We broke into their armoury. All the weapons are over there."

It doesn't take long to find the ZX90. Troya examines it.

"It is the right material," she says, "but we will need a lot more than this sample if we are to correct the Somnolents' genetic fault. We need industrial quantities."

"So we go to Metakal and get it," I say.

My words send a groan around the room.

"What's the problem?"

"Metakal is a Cerberus stronghold," Yrin explains. "It's a frontier planet. The rule of law doesn't reach places like that. The last three sheriffs have died trying to clean up the planet. We'd be marching into the gates of Hell."

"Is there any alternative?" Azari asks.

It is a long time before Yrin answers.

"No," he says.

"OK, gates of Hell it is."

Six

We take one of the Jumeli's sprint battleships. We are carrying enough of the Jumeli's hoard to pay for all the Metakyprosium we need. The thought of a whole race of fighters like Yrin fills me with hope. We complete the journey to Metakal in three days. While the battleship orbits the planet, a small party of us land in the shuttle we had taken from Thren 15. Yrin leads the group. There is Azari, Troya and the surly Arachnibrid. For some reason Yrin has a high opinion of the dark, spiky-skinned, eight-legged warrior. In a fight, Yrin says, we will be able to rely on him. I make the mistake of asking his name. He turns eight intense eyes my way.

"The Archnibrid does not waste time on names," he growls.

"What if you want to talk about another Arachnibrid?" I ask. "I mean, how do you refer to him?"

"I don't."

"But...."

Yrin catches my eye. He is advising me to drop it. The Arachnibrid stamps off in the direction of the blinking lights in the distance.

"What's wrong with him?" I ask.

"You asked how he talks to another Arachnibrid," Azari explains. "There are no more. He is the last of his kind. When he dies, his race is extinct."

I stare at the spiny back and start after him.

"I'm going to apologise."

"You weren't to know. Leave him be."

"How did it happen?"

"Cerberus happened. The Arachnibrids were the most social race in the galaxy. They lived in a giant nest on their home planet. They travelled from clan to clan on colossal cobwebs. They did not venture out of their home territory. They did not trade. They needed nothing from anyone. They had lived that way for centuries. They feared nobody. It was a kind of spidery paradise."

"So what changed?"

Yrin starts to doze and I give him a nudge.

"Engineers discovered huge deposits of minerals on the Arachnibrids' home planet. A front company set up by Cerberus tried to negotiate a mining treaty. The Arachnibrids rejected the offer. They had everything they needed. Why would they want to change a way of life that had served them well since the dawn of time. They refused to give permission to the mining company."

I sense what's coming next.

"Cerberus agents planted a series of huge explosive devices under the Arachnibrids' nest. They mowed down any survivors as they emerged." He nodded in the direction of our companion. "He alone was able to get away."

"He told you this?"

Yrin shakes his head.

"He will not talk about the fate of his people. He has only opened his heart to one other being. Troya. Her people were hunted in similar fashion. She is the one he told."

I glance at the apeling scientist.

"We were in the same work gang for months," she explains. "I used to tell him about the way my people had been exterminated so they could log the forest. Finally, he told me his story."

"What does he want? Revenge?"

Troya shakes her head.

"Beneath their spiky exteriors the Arachnibrids were a peaceful race. He wants justice. He knows that depends on President Shavlotan. In the struggle for peace we will have no firmer friend."

I watch the Arachnibrid trudging steadily toward the town. I find myself wondering how he carries on, but there are no words capable of saying what I want to. We fall in behind him and approach the dimly lit streets. Suddenly Azari hisses a warning.

"Stop!"

The Arachnibrid halts and gives her a questioning look.

"Not here. Look"

She indicates a faint line in the earth.

"Take one step further and we will set off an alarm. There must be a reason the townsfolk don't allow visitors at night."

Yrin examines the perimeter line. "It might be more than an alarm. We might set off some kind of lethal defensive weapon. Looks like we'll have to sleep under the stars and wait for the morning."

I find myself searching the darkness for movement. "But what are they keeping out? I don't like this."

The Arachnibrid stares bleakly into the gloom. "You're right to be nervous. Metakal has a bad reputation. There are three reasons to come here and only three reasons. One, you want to make a fast buck out of the Metakyprosium mines. Two, you want to get away from the law."

"And the third?" Azari asks.

"The reason I volunteered for this mission," the Arachnibrid grunts. "You want to die, but you're too much of a coward to kill yourself."

"You don't care whether you live or die?"

"I care *how* I live or die, and what for. I care about leaving this universe a better place than when I entered it. The screams of millions of my kind drive me on. I hear them in my dreams. I want to break the power of Cerberus and its allies. I will happily die for that." Before anyone can speak, he stares us down. "I will take first watch. I will wake the humanoid in an hour and a half. Then you Azari, Yrin, Troya in that order."

I notice that he calls everyone by their name except me. Cerberus is an alliance of many races, but humans like me lead it. No wonder he can't say my name. The Arachnibrid expects us to sleep while he broods on the fate of his lost spider-people, but I lie in my sleeping bag, tossing and turning, starting at every sound. I know we are not alone. The darkness does not just have eyes. It has claws, fangs, hunger. I have sensed it ever since we came across that defensive line. We are in great danger. I don't know its nature. I don't know its form. But it is there, in the heart of the night, waiting. After ninety minutes of uneasy dozing, I feel the Arachnibrid's spiny touch.

"It is your turn, humanoid."

I nod. As the Archnibrid spreads himself on the earth, I wander over to the gnarled trunk of a tree and peer into the night. Mist swirls in from the swamps to the east. It is hard to make out anything in the shifting murk, but I know they're there, the creatures this perimeter has been built to exclude. As I lean on the tree trunk examining my surroundings, I feel dizzy at the thought of where that first meeting with Liesl Schlachthof has brought me. Everything is so strange, yet oddly normal. Stranger that I am, it is as if there is some buried memory of these planets two centuries in the future and half a universe away from home. Cerberus the game has prepared me well. Cerberus the conspiracy may yet destroy me.

I am still musing on my strange fate when I hear a sound like wind rustling through swamp grass. I find myself turning, expecting to feel a cool night breeze on my cheeks. Instead, I see a landscape quite still and windless. So what is that noise? I squint as I strain to see something in the muddy darkness. What is that noise? Then I have it. It is bare feet racing through the rushes and the tangles of weed.

"Wake up!" I shout urgently.

I see Troya's huge eyes staring questioningly.

"Somebody's coming."

Within moments my comrades are on their feet. Sleepy eyes blink into the gloom. Weapons are primed.

"Do you hear them?" I ask, my voice shaking.

"We all hear them," Yrin says grimly. "We are under attack."

Presently the night begins to tremble. Planes of darkness flutter. It's them, our attackers. Azari takes a few steps forward.

"Use the Night Bloom," she orders. "There."

I twist the barrel of the ZX90 and the darkness melts away. Scores, hundreds of greyish figures are swarming over the marshy ground before us, kicking up the stinking mud.

"Rapid fire!" Yrin yells, powering up his pulse rifle.

Instantly our fire is ripping great holes in the seething mass of clay-like forms as they advance. In spite of the withering fire that is thinning their ranks the creatures continue to advance. Not one of them hesitates, wavers or retreats. We continue to pump blasts of energy into the tsunami of living flesh. Still they fall. Still they advance. For the first time I see their faces and my blood runs cold. Their eyes start from their eye sockets. Their finned, clawed hands are raised, ready to slash at us should they get close enough. Their mouths gape open, howling and shrieking.

"What are they?"

I turn to look at Yrin, but he is sinking to his knees, eyes closed.

"Not now!" I yell.

Yrin's eyelids flutter and he scrambles back to his feet.

"Did you ask me something?" Yrin asks, knuckling his eyes.

"What are those things?"

"Swamp runners," Yrin tells me. "I've seen these creatures on planets all across the Lycan-Thyperidean asteroid belt. The swamps are infested with their gelatinous spawn. They squirm free in their hundreds or thousands and hunt human flesh.

"They've got no fear," I gasp as they come ever closer.

"They hunt. They eat. They create more of their hideous breed. That is all they do."

We must have mown down hundreds. That leaves scores of survivors and still they come. In a matter of seconds they will be upon us.

"Keep firing on them as they advance," he orders. "Leave it to me and the Arichnibrid to deal with the front runners."

One of the swamp runners is several metres ahead of the rest. Yrin smashes him to the ground. Three more hurl themselves at us. Yrin snaps the neck of one. The Arachnibrid feeds the other two into his enormous jaws. For all our efforts the grey tide of the swamp runners continues to surge forward.

"We can't kill them all!" I cry.

"Stand firm!" Azari snaps.

Her words have barely died away when powerful lights snap on behind us. I glimpse silhouetted figures out of the corner of my eye. Cannon fire thunders tearing through what remains of the swamp runners. The tattered survivors slip away into the night. We turn to face our rescuers. One of the shadowy forms steps forward, marking her out as their leader.

"Who the hell are you?" she roars. "What do you think you're doing, stirring up the swamp runners?"

We hear the town's defenders priming their weapons.

"You'd better have a good explanation," the leader continues, "or you die where you stand."

Seven

The leader of the townspeople taps a code into a keypad on the back of her glove.

"Enter the perimeter," she commands. "I want to take a good luck at the dumb skrits who have brought a full-scale swamp runner attack down on our heads."

For the first time I am able to make out her features. She is tall, as human as me or Liesl Schlachthof. Her long, black hair falls in a braid down her back. Unlike the ragtag militia assembled around her, she goes without a helmet. Even her body armour is light. She is swathed entirely in black with a protective jacket covering her back and chest. She looks no older than her late twenties, but something in her eyes hints that she is older. She surveys us one by one.

"This is an odd combination," she says. "An Azaal, a Somnolent, an Archnibrid, an apeling and...you." She leans closer. "You're a bit young to be getting up to no good out here on this godforsaken lump of rock."

"I'm not getting up to anything," I protest. "We're here to trade."

She seems amused. "Trade? What have you got to trade?"

Yrin nudges Troya. "Show her the sample."

Troya goes to swing her backpack off her right shoulder.

"Not so fast!" barks a heavily armed militiaman. He has a prehensile trunk that pokes through an intimidating full-face mask. "Don't trust them, Xeda."

I glance at the leader. Now we have a name.

"I don't trust anyone," Xeda retorts. "I wouldn't survive long out here if I did. Scan the bag."

The scan reveals nothing dangerous. Xeda acknowledges the fact then turns to Troya.

"Open it."

Troya reveals the precious stones. Xeda examines them. She tries to look casual, but her body language says she is seriously impressed by the quality of the gems.

"Take them to the lab. I want them valued."

"Now I know what you have to offer. What do you want from me?"

"Metakyprosium," Yrin says. "As much as you've got."

Xeda examines Yrin's face for a few moments then she gives an order.

"Take their weapons. Give them a thorough body search then bring them to my quarters."

The thorough body search sounds scary, but it consists of walking through a portal of silvery light. It's the cordon at the Presidential Palace again. It takes a matter of seconds. Once Xeda's guards are satisfied that we're not packing hidden weapons, they march us back into her presence. Her quarters are a plain room with a few tables and chairs and a large multi-screen display of different views from the township. Xeda's gauntlet buzzes. She flips open a patch and watches a visual.

"It appears I am dealing with notorious fugitives," she announces. For some reason, she seems to find it funny. She presses a key and a hologram appears.

"Yrin Gok," she says. "Somnolent. Aided and abetted the escape of a known terrorist."

She brings up a second image.

"Azari Azaal," she says. "Suspected Azaal terrorist. Filmed participating in the assassination attempt on President Shavlotan."

I wonder why neither Yrin nor Azari are protesting their innocence.

"Henry Kwok. Known terrorist and accomplice in the assassination attempt."

"It isn't true," I cry. "They framed me."

"Yes, you would say that." She reads the files of Troya and the Arachnibrid. "Now what are you two doing in this company? A distinguished scientist, last seen when her disabled ship drifted into the Razono Vozela."

"We took a direct hit from an asteroid," Troya says. "We were unlucky, that's all."

"And you?" Xeda asks, staring into the Arachnibrid's eight black eyes.

"They want to destroy Cerberus," the Arachnibrid answers. "I want to destroy Cerberus. That's all there is to it."

"But the broadcasts coming out of Thren 15 say your friends here are part of the Cerberus conspiracy against the President."

Yrin finally speaks up. "It looks bad," he says, "but we were trying to thwart the assassination attempt. Run the footage again. You can see that Azari saved the President's life. The real assassin is in the corner of the shot."

Xeda laughs. "I know what happened. My guys already did an analysis of the sequence of events."

"You know!" I explode. "So why put us through the third degree?"

"It's just my way," Xeda says. She leans forward. "Look, you are either very brave or very stupid. Metakal is crawling with Cerberus agents. When you stopped the assassination attempt you didn't exactly sever the first head of Cerberus. Let's say you muzzled it. But what do you do next? You march straight into one of its strongholds. The second head of Cerberus might just have vicious teeth."

"But you're in charge here, aren't you?"

Xeda looks at me as if I just crawled out from under a stone.

"In charge, is that what you think? I have been sheriff of Metakal for two years. No other law officer has lived this long. The average survival rate is six months. I have been involved in over twenty shoot-outs with Cerberus agents. I have been the target of ten assassination attempts. Does that sound like I'm in charge?" She shifts her gaze from me to Yrin, then to each of our group in turn. "I'm just about surviving here. Look, I'm on your side, but I don't understand why you're here looking for Metakyprosium."

Yrin explains. Xeda listens.

"You really think you can turn the Somnolents into an army?" she asks. "I do."

"That's hard to swallow," Xeda says. "You do know your kind is the laughing stock of the whole galaxy. I mean, warriors that fall asleep in the heat of battle. It doesn't inspire much confidence, does it?"

She glances at Yrin, expecting an answer, but he is snoring loudly.

"See what I mean?"

"Should I wake him?" I ask.

"No," Xeda says. "Let him sleep. Where is the rest of this hoard you want to exchange for Metakyprosium?"

"Our ship is orbiting Metakal," Troya answers. "Once the terms of the exchange are made, we will prepare to dock with the vessel delivering the consignment of Metakyprosium."

"Do you think Cerberus is onto you?"

Azari shrugs.

"Who knows? We've been on the run since the attack on the President."

We talk for another ten minutes. Finally, Xeda comes to a decision.

"I'll let you have the Metakyprosium," she says. "But the moment news of the hoard gets round, every scumbag on the planet is going to be thinking of ways to get his tentacles on it. You've just made a lawless frontier town even more dangerous than it already is." She rubs her nose. "Wake Sleeping Beauty. I'll show you round the place."

Metakal Town by day is pretty much the same as Metakal Town by night. The thick, muddy darkness has been replaced by thin, muddy light. Shuttles and space freighters come in slowly over the jagged mountains and flat, stagnant swamps. The streets are heaving with outlaws from a dozen star systems. I steal glances at them, wondering what crimes they've committed. I get the odd snarl, but most of them pass by without giving me a second glance. Xeda nods in the direction of a huddle of reptilian creatures squatting on the steps of a bar.

"Geccans," she says. "They've spent the last twelve hours getting high on Metakyprosium dust. They're quiet now. Once the effects kick in they will be challenging every life form in town to a fight to the death."

"Why don't you ban the dust?" Azari asks.

"It is banned," Xeda answers. "There's no problem making the laws. Enforcing them is the difficult bit."

A translucent Skellit glides past. These creatures always give me an uncomfortable feeling. It's not just that they are hard to see. Their body seems to merge into objects, sliding through them like a kind of hot jelly.

"Sheriff," he grunts.

Xeda doesn't return the greeting.

"He spoke to you," I say.

"I heard," Xeda said. "He's tried to kill me twice already. I don't feel like passing the time of day with him."

"So why isn't he in prison?" I ask.

Xeda laughs.

"I can't get any proof," she explains. "That Skellit is head of the Cerberus Chapter here in Metakal. Poses as a businessman. He never gets his hands dirty, but his hoods are behind most of the trouble around town."

I watch the Skellit as he seems to dissolve into the grainy half-light.

"Does he have a name?"

"That's Don Menchi. If he gets wind of your plans there's going to be a war."

I try to get a bead on Don Menchi, but he has vanished into the drab morning light.

Eight

The grey mist doesn't clear all that morning. We eat with Xeda in her office. I realise that all her guards are pachyderm-humanoid hybrids like the one I saw earlier. They stand guard, small, colourless eyes peering out of the window, ears twitching apprehensively at each sound. Occasionally their trunks stiffen and they take deep breaths of the stale air before relaxing as they recognise the scent of the passer-by.

"Do you always have this much security?" Azari asks.

"Every moment of every day," Xeda answers, her voice weary with stress. "Whether I am in the bathroom or in bed I am always armed. I never have fewer than three guards in attendance."

"Even in the bathroom?"

"Not *in* the bathroom, you dumb skrit! Outside the door. Don't you know a lady when you see one?"

I did, but after that outburst I might just be changing my mind. I'm wondering what to say next when I notice that every pachyderm guard is breathing my scent.

"They don't suspect *me!*"

Xeda snaps her fingers impatiently at the pachyderms. "They suspect everybody. That's how we stay alive."

She wipes her mouth with the back of her hand. Lady she might be, but the rough and ready habits of the frontier have rubbed off on her.

"Are you ready to go out to the MK mines?" she asks.

By MK she means Metakyprosium. Everyone is ready with the exception of Yrin Gok. He is snoring away with his head on his plate. When we wake him there are ribbons of pasta and streaks of sauce in his hair. One of the pachyderms vacuums it up.

"Thank you," Yrin says. "I think."

The pachyderms fan out on the verandah outside Xeda's HQ. They train their weapons on the street, alleys and rooftops. One of them hands his weapons to a comrade and checks the vehicle chassis for explosive devices. He takes a scanner from his belt and sweeps the road for mines.

"We're clear."

A command crackles. "Go, go, go."

That's the signal for us to race across the dirt road and board our vehicles. The Arachnibrid joins most of the pachyderms in the lead vehicle. Yrin joins two more in the rear. The rest of us take our places next to Xeda in the middle transport. She waves and the convoy roars out of town in a cloud of dust. We move fast, powerful engines thrumming. Pulse cannons target the buildings as we flash past.

"Is this how you have to travel?" Troya asks.

Xeda nods.

"Yes, it's pretty stressful. You need plenty of R and R to cope with life out here."

"Where do you go?" I ask.

"I don't."

"But you said...."

"Look, I said you need R and R to survive. One problem, there's nobody to take my place and people aren't exactly queuing up to replace me. I haven't had a break in two years and I'm on duty 36/8."

"Don't you mean 24/7?"

"I know how many hours and days there are on Metakal," Xeda snorts.

I'm feeling like a dumb skrit again. By now we have crossed the causeway over the swamp and we are on the open plain. The mist is getting thicker.

"Pull down your visors," Xeda tells us. "They help with the visibility."

Suddenly the lead vehicle slows. Xeda puts her finger to her earpiece.

"What is it?" She listens to the reply. "Slopgrot!"

"Something wrong?"

"There's an MK tanker blocking the highway up ahead. Looks like ambush time."

One of the pachyderms snorts a comment. "It's Cerberus."

The convoy vehicles slew across the road. The guards swing the pulse cannons on their tripods. The only sound is the snuffling of the wind across the bleak terrain.

"They're watching us all right."

I squint through the murk. "I don't see anything."

"Keep your eyes on the drainage channels. That's where they're going to come from."

The uneasy silence continues. I go to speak, but Xeda shakes her head. She seems to have seen something. She holds up three fingers and indicates one of the drainage channels. The nearest guard nods and sniffs with his trunk. His thumb powers up his rifle.

"Go!"

Xeda's voice crackles through the air. She springs from the vehicle and races towards the channel. The guards are moving fast. I glance at Azari. She shrugs and springs down. The pulse cannons are laying down covering fire. Dirt, dust and shards of clay spray around us. There are loud explosions overhead.

"We're under fire!" Azari warns.

"You don't say!"

We are closing on the channel. I can see dark shapes in the dust. I twist the grip of the ZX90 and the Night Bloom illuminates the scene. Xeda's fighters take down half a dozen of the Cerberus ambushers. As quickly as it started the firefight is over. Shadowy forms retreat down the channels. In the eerie silence that follows, we glance at each other. I twist round to make my way back to the transport. In the same instant I glimpse movement out of the corner of my eye. My spine tingles. There's a surviving Cerberus gunman and he's got a bead on me. There is no time to dive for cover or return fire. I am numb with horror.

"Down!"

There is a sudden blur and I am chewing dust. After that everything moves at breakneck speed. I feel myself being roughly bundled onto the back seat of my transport.

"What happened?" I gasp, my heart still pounding.

"I pulled you out of the goon's line of fire," Xeda explains. "Azari dealt with the sniper."

I stare at Azari. "I owe you my life."

"Forget it," she says. "Next time, don't turn your back until you know we're completely clear."

My neck burns.

"I won't screw up again."

We reach the mining camp without further incident. The MK comes out of huge opencaste mines. I stare at the giant diggers mauling the ore out of the ruined ground. Xeda strides across the ground, picks up a lump of ore and tosses it to Troya.

"That's your MK."

Troya examines it.

"Is it ready for shipping?"

Xeda nods. "We'll load it immediately. The sooner we get the MK, and you, out of here the better."

The diggers are piling MK into a pair of containers. Another machine presses the material down. While the diggers and the compactor load the containers, we sit around in the dust, weapons primed. Yrin presses a pair of fingers to his eyes.

"Keep them peeled, Henry. There are plenty more Cerberus agents out there. We took down seven on my count. There could be another fifteen or twenty watching us now. My gaze travels over the flat, featureless land. I imagine danger waiting in every hollow, death lurking behind every boulder.

"It's always like this," Xeda grumbles. "You get a few minutes of white-hot terror then hours of waiting. They hope the boredom will wear you down. Then, bam, they launch another attack. I have to get lucky every day. They only have to get lucky once.

"When will you get away?" I ask.

"The only way I leave this place is in a sealed box," Xeda says ruefully.

Presently one of the guards rises to his feet. One of his comrades is squatting on his haunches. He sees the movement.

"What's wrong?"

"Energy ripple," the pachyderm answers. "They're preparing another attack."

Xeda nods. "Keep your eyes peeled, people." She marches over to the miners. "How long?"

There is a grunted answer. "Fifteen minutes. Twenty tops."

Xeda gives an impatient snort. "You've got ten or nobody gets paid." She catches my eye. "It's the only language these guys understand."

By now my skin is crawling. We have survived one firefight, but there is worse to come. Most of the Cerberus raiding party survived the last skirmish. They are crouching in the channels, biding their time. We are out in the open and everybody is feeling vulnerable.

"Five minutes!" Xeda shouts to the miners.

"Why's she telling the ambushers our plans?" I demand.

"They're determined to stop the shipment," Troya explains. "They've got wind of what we're doing. Xeda's trying to provoke an attack. Better here than on the open road to town."

106

Xeda's idea bears fruit soon enough. There is movement in the channels. "Here we go!"

When the attack finally begins it is beyond anything we could have imagined.

"They've got a Behemoth!" Xeda yells, alerted to the telltale growl of a giant field weapon.

"Behemoth?" I ask. "What the hell is that?"

Azari taps my shoulder. "See for yourself."

I follow her pointing finger and groan. "You've got to be kidding!"

Cerberus' secret weapon is a giant digger. It is perfectly designed for the deep canals and channels that criss-crossed Metakal's open plains. It is a huge mechanical serpent, slithering across the ground on links of flexible steel bands. The fiery eyes are giant laser beams, the yawning mouth constructed of two powerful steel jaws. I swallow hard.

"How are we supposed to fight that?"

Ominously, nobody has an answer. We stand transfixed, staring at the Behemoth as it towers above us.

Azari glances at Xeda. "You obviously know something about this thing."

"It's a piece of mining equipment," Xeda explains. "The companies send them into deep mines. But this one is armed."

"It looks like Cerberus has shipped it in as essential mining equipment," one of the guards observes. "But how did Don Menchi smuggle those cannons past customs."

Xeda snorts. "Ten thousand credits will buy you any customs officer on the planet."

A mechanical voice brays across the plain.

"Withdraw."

Nobody moves.

"Leave the Metakyprosium and pull back to town. If you do not obey you will be destroyed."

"No MK, no revival of the Magenti," Yrin says grimly. "No revival of the Magenti, no opposition to Cerberus. No opposition to Cerberus, no peace. No...."

"OK, OK," Xeda says, interrupting him. "We get it, all right. We've got to fight, but how do we fight that. It is designed to survive the stresses of deep mining. Our pulse cannons are useless against its armour."

For a few seconds the Behemoth's head sways back and forth.

"You have ten seconds," the mechanical voice informs us. "Ten, nine, eight...."

The guards start to fire. Their pulse cannons are as ineffective as Xeda warned.

"Seven, six, five, four...."

Yrin states the obvious. "Somehow we have to protect the ore."

"Three...."

"But how?"

"Two, one."

Searing laser beams rake the earth in front of us. A jet of flame engulfs our lead vehicle. It explodes in a fireball. Two guards somersault through the air, dead before they hit the ground. Suddenly everybody is firing. They know their weapons are useless, but they are determined to resist, even if it is symbolic.

"How much MK have we got?" Troya demands.

"90% of the consignment," one of the miners answers.

"It's enough," Troya says. "Let's get out of here."

Now everybody is scrambling into the transports. We roar away, bouncing down the track through a wall of flame and smoke.

"How fast does that thing go?" I ask.

Xeda consults her glove screen. "Two hundred and twenty kilometres an hour max."

"And these vehicles?"

There is a long silence.

"Two hundred."

"You're kidding?"

"I don't joke about survival. I gave you the good news."

Yrin frowns.

"The Behemoth is faster than us. How is that the good news?"

"We can do two hundred with no load. Pulling the MK containers that's down to 180."

"Oh, Slopgrot!"

"Quite."

I glance back. The Behemoth is closing fast. The steel jaws snap, once, twice, then there's a sickening, grinding squeal of metal accompanied by the agonised shrieks of the dying. The Behemoth has taken out the rear vehicle.

"Slopgrot!" Yrin snaps. "That's half the MK."

I twist in my seat. The Behemoth is crunching the twisted remains of the transport, but the MK container is intact, though on its side.

"No," I tell them. "The container has survived."

Everybody stares.

Xeda peers through the smoke. "We can hook it up to the back of our container. It will slow us down, but it's possible."

Yrin doesn't need any more encouragement. He leaps from his seat and pounds towards the container, rocking it back and forth to set it on its wheels. While he struggles to right it shards of twisted metal fall from the Behemoth's mouth. Now and then Yrin glimpses the shower of debris and shifts right or left to avoid it.

"Reverse," Xeda orders. "He's nearly ready."

That's when the Behemoth's operator sees what's happening. Lasers blaze and a ring of flame dances around us. The heat is intense.

"Yrin!"

The smoke clears for a second and we can see him hauling the wheeled container towards us. Azari springs down and cranks open the mechanism to attach the second container.

"It's no use," the Arachnibrid growls. "We're at their mercy. The Behemoth can take us whenever it wants. Is there no weakness?"

Troya runs a scan.

"There may be one," she says.

"Where?"

She indicates the scarlet eyes.

"A pulse cannon fired at point blank range might just shatter those windows."

"Pass the cannon," the Arachnibrid orders. "I am the only one who can climb the Behemoth carrying the cannon."

There's no arguing with that. Nobody else has eight legs.

"You can't," Troya cries. "If you release pulse energy that close, it will destroy you as well."

The Arachnibrid shrugs.

"I am one alone. Maybe this is my destiny, the last act of my kind. If it helps stop Cerberus it will be worthwhile."

Nobody tries to dissuade him. He is right. It is destiny. Either he dies or we all do. He snatches the cannon from its tripod and scampers towards the oncoming Behemoth, zigzagging to avoid the flickering lasers.

"He's on the Behemoth," I report.

I see him climbing with purpose and agility. Too late, the Behemoth sees the danger. It starts to writhe and twist, desperate to dislodge the Arachnibrid, but he clings on.

"Drive!" Xeda yells.

"We can't just go and leave him," Troya pleads.

"What good is it going to do to watch him die?"

Xeda is blunt. There isn't a single iota of sentimentality. The MK is key to defeating Cerberus. That is all that matters. As our transport roars away she keeps her eyes on the road ahead. The rest of us take our cue from her. Nobody wants to see the Arachnibrid's end. Troya alone strains to see her friend. We have been roaring down the track for less than ninety seconds when there is an ear-splitting explosion. Shock waves rock the containers, but they remain attached. I glimpse Troya's face. Apeling eyes don't form tears, but they are weeping.

On we drive. Soon the shock waves subside and the dust settles. We scream into town and stop outside Xeda's HQ. Don Menchi is watching from across the road.

"Had some trouble, Miss Xeda," he asks.

She wipes away the dirt and the dust with the back of her hand and strides into her office.

"Not so you'd notice," she calls over her shoulder.

I inspect Don Menchi's cold features, expecting to see some sign of disappointment. His face is a mask.

"Forget about him," Yrin advises. "He has thrown everything at us and we're still standing."

My gaze doesn't leave Don Menchi's eyes. There is something about that rigid stare that tells me he isn't done with us yet.

Nine

The orbiting ship knows we are ready. Yrin has started loading the MK ore. Nobody speaks. The Arachnibrid's fate hangs over us like the smog that haunts Metakal. I wander to the edge of the airstrip. The town is quiet. There are a few reptilians high on MK dust squatting on the street. Don Menchi stands impassively by his transport, unblinking eyes fixed on our ship. I wonder what he is thinking. Somehow, I can't bring myself to believe that he has accepted defeat.

"Something wrong?"

It's Xeda.

"It's Don Menchi," I tell her. "He just stands there watching."

Xeda follows the direction of my stare. "Ignore him."

Her words are brave enough, but there is something in her voice, a hesitation, a buzz of concern. She is worried. As she walks away she whispers something to her guards. Soon there are three of them patrolling the edge of the strip, weapons at the ready. Xeda approaches Yrin.

"Is there no way of speeding this up?"

"Azari is running the final checks. We'll be ready to go in ten."

Xeda is impatient. "Minutes or hours?"

Yrin snorts. "What's your hurry?"

"I just want to see the last of your ugly mug."

Yrin nods. "I thought it was something like that."

The wind is picking up, gusting across the plain and scouring the streets of the town. Otherwise it is quiet. A deathly stillness hangs over the lonely street. Any moment I expect to see Cerberus goons pouring from the buildings and raking the airstrip with fire. But nothing happens. Don Menchi continues to watch. He doesn't move. There is no expression on his face. What's he waiting for?

"We're ready," Azari announces.

It takes me by surprise. The expected firefight as the Cerberus chapter tries to prevent our departure doesn't materialise. We've done it. We say our goodbyes to Xeda and board. The engines hum. A cloud of dust swallows Xeda and her pachyderm guards. We rise steadily into the air.

"Why did he let us go without a fight?" I murmur.

"What's that?" Azari asks, shaking Yrin out of his latest doze.

"Don Menchi. He didn't try to stop us."

"Were you not there when Cerberus tried to gun us down? Have you forgotten about the Behemoth?"

"I haven't forgotten anything," I tell her. "But there are a lot more Cerberus agents on Metakal. Xeda said so. Why didn't they launch an attack? We were sitting ducks. It doesn't make any sense."

Yrin shrugs. "Maybe they got a taste of our firepower."

By now we are entering space. In less than an hour we will be docking with the mother ship. Troya enters the cabin. She has been silent since the Arachnibrid's sacrifice. She senses our unease.

"Is there a problem?"

Azari nods in my direction.

"Henry thinks there is."

Troya tilts her head.

"What is it?"

"I don't know," I tell her. "It's just a feeling."

I explain my misgivings. To my surprise, Troya takes me seriously.

"Did you sweep the ship?" she asks.

"What?'

"Did you run a security sweep?"

"There was no time," Azari says. "We had to get the ship in the sky before Cerberus launched another attack. Why, what's on your mind?"

"We've all been distracted," Troya explains. "Our minds were on the attack or on getting the MK loaded. What if the danger wasn't from a Cerberus attack from outside, but from within."

"What are you saying?"

Troya waves her hand. "The ship. It's been standing on the strip. Who's been guarding it?"

Suddenly I am not the only one who is concerned.

"Run a systems check," Azari says urgently. "Fuel systems. Life support. Docking mechanism. Everything."

The scan has only been running for a few seconds when an alarm wails. Azari runs to a screen.

"What is it?"

"Life forms. Three of them. They're in the docking bay."

"Can we get a visual?"

Azari hits a button and we are staring at surveillance footage of the docking bay.

Three disturbingly familiar forms are making their way through a hatch door. I recognise the insane stares, the feral hunger in the inhuman expressions.

"Swamp runners!"

Yrin reaches for a weapon. Azari shakes her head.

"Are you crazy? We can't use our weapons on board ship. One misdirected shot and we're dust fragments drifting in space."

That means hand-to-hand fighting. The thought makes my blood run cold. I remember the slick, silvery-grey skin, the eyes that started from their sockets, the finned, clawed hands that slashed and ripped, the desperation to maim and kill. Now there were three of the creatures on the loose aboard ship...and they were coming our way.

"Can't we just lock them out?" I ask.

Azari nods. "There's nothing to fear."

Troya interrupts. "I don't think that's strictly true."

"What do you mean?"

"Look at the surveillance footage. The doors to the docking bay are always kept locked. Who opened them?"

Yrin turns. "Are you saying there's a traitor among us?"

Troya shakes her head. "I'm saying that whoever introduced the swamp runners to the ship has rigged the doors to open on command.

"It's Don Menchi," I say. "He's controlling the doors from the surface of Metakal."

Troya nods. "Sounds a reasonable assumption. He's probably watching the scene on a screen in the comfort of his quarters."

Yrin scowls. "He's expecting to see us ripped apart by those monsters. Let's not give him the satisfaction."

"Meaning?"

"We don't sit here waiting for them to come to us. We go to them. Who's with me?"

Azari steps forward, Troya too.

"No," Yrin says. "You know how to process the MK. You stay here."

That leaves me. Three onto three. Not great odds.

"We're not really going to fight them hand to hand, are we?"

Yrin opens a weapons store. "We can't use pulse rifles," he answers. "We can't use that ZX90 either. We could puncture the shell of the spacecraft then we all die. This is the best thing we've got."

He hands me what looks like a silver pole. I give him a questioning stare. "Repulsion prods," he explains. "We use them in close combat. They deliver one hell of a shock and repel most life forms weighing less than

114

a hundred kilos."

"Most?"

I stare at the prod and frown.

"Something wrong?"

Until I set foot on Metakal everything seemed familiar. The Cerberus game had prepared me well. Suddenly everything is new and strange. Liesl Schlachthof obviously expected me to be dead or in prison by now. She did nothing to prepare me for anything after the assassination attempt.

"Nothing wrong," I say. "

Armed with Yrin's feeble reassurances, we open the cabin door and step into the dimly lit corridors. We move slowly, systematically examining each recess, each room, each hatch. We have just opened up a heating duct when a feral shriek echoes down the corridor. Yrin activates his prod. Azari follows suit.

"Will these things work?" I ask.

"They pack one hell of a punch," Yrin answers. "That's all I can tell you. How effective they will be against the swamp runners I can only guess." That's when the first swamp runner springs from the darkness. Yrin jabs the prod into its chest. The creature tumbles to the floor, twisting and writhing. Before Yrin can move in for the kill a second of the creatures bursts from a hatch. Azari blocks its attack with her shoulder and uses its momentum to slam it into the wall. While my comrades battle the runner attacks, I move uneasily forward, searching for some sign of the third. I edge round the next corner and howl with terror. I have walked straight into the waiting runner. It crashes its head into my face and I stumble backwards, blood spilling from my nose, the creature's glutinous spittle pebbling my face. Pain fizzes through my shoulder. The monster has slashed my arm. Blinded by pain I swing the prod, hoping to get lucky.

"Henry! Down!"

It is Azari's voice.

I crumple to the floor. Something hisses past my left ear and there is an ear-splitting scream. When my senses finally start to clear I see that Azari has driven the prod through the runner's eye socket and into its brain.

"Thanks," I pant, struggling to staunch the blood. "Did you get the other two?"

Azari nods. Yrin is already dragging the corpses to an expulsion tube.

"The danger is past," she tells me. "Leave Yrin to it. Let's get back to Troya."

The moment we enter the cabin and see the expression on Troya's face, I know it isn't over.

"Now what?"

"Don Menchi has played us for fools," Troya groans.

Azari looks confused. "I don't understand. We've destroyed the swamp runners."

"Don't you get it? They were a distraction. They were designed to divert our attention from the main danger."

"Which is?"

Troya points to a screen. "In all the chaos I almost missed it. We were meant to discover the swamp runners. What we weren't meant to see...was this."

I try to make sense of what I'm saying. "Do you mean that hotspot?"

"That hotspot," Troya answers, "is a bomb. We've got less than two minutes until it blows. It's hopeless."

Strangely, I feel like laughing. Has Cerberus inadvertently trained me to defuse their bomb?

"Maybe not," I say. "Where is the device?"

Troya gives me the information I need. I sprint from the room almost colliding with Yrin. I have been a liability so far. Now I can put that right. Within forty-five seconds I am working on a Neutron Mine identical to the one Liesl Schlachthof brought into my home. Azari catches up with me.

116

"Can you disarm it?"

I chuckle. "I already did."

"But that red light is still winking."

"Don't worry about it," I say. "I've bypassed the main current."

"But why not disarm it completely, jettison it into space."

I shake my head.

"That can wait. This way, Don Menchi will think we're dead. It will buy us some time."

"Very clever," Azari says, impressed.

I smile, imagining Don Menchi's face when he discovers he's been tricked. "Aren't I just?"

Ten

The journey back through the Razono Vozela is an interlude, a calm intermission between the relentless attacks of Cerberus on Metakal and the fate that awaits us back on Thren 15 as we try to behead the conspiracy. I don't see much of Troya. She is spending every waking moment processing the MK ore to develop an antidote to the Somnolents' condition.

I pass my time running and re-running footage of the scene outside the Presidential Palace. With Azari's help I am able to put together a sequence of images. There is Liesl entering the square. I follow her progress through the crowd, then there she is again making her way inside the inner security cordon. Finally, there is the dramatic footage of her assassination attempt and Azari's desperate, last minute intervention to save the President's life.

"This is the woman who recruited you?" she asks.

I gaze at the eyes that transfixed me and nod ruefully.

"I was stupid. It felt like a great adventure. She flattered me. Man, I was dumb."

"Don't be hard on yourself." Azari tells me. "Cerberus is a formidable foe.

It has made fools of us all."

Just how formidable Cerberus really is we will discover in a few hours. I am still examining the footage of the assassination attempt when Troya enters the control room with Yrin.

"It's ready," she says. "Do you want to try it?"

Yrin nods eagerly. "What do I have to do?"

"Just stand still."

Troya is holding what looks like a small pistol. Instead of a gun barrel there is a circular pad bristling with needles.

"What are you going to do with that?" Yrin demands.

His gaze never leaves the contraption in Troya's hand.

"Inject you, of course."

"You're going to stick that in me! No way. What do you think I am, some kind of Scringedangle?"

"Of course I'm going to stick it into you. That's how we usually inject people."

Yrin's eyes are huge and scared. I am surprised to see the self-proclaimed great warrior trembling like a leaf.

"Will it hurt?"

Troya examines her giant patient with a wry smile on her face. "Yrin, you claim to be the fiercest warrior in the galaxy. How can you be afraid of a little needle?"

"There are lots of little needles there," Yrin objects. "There is also a very big needle in the middle."

"Do you want to be cured?" Troya asks impatiently.

Yrin still isn't happy. "Yes, I suppose so. Are there any side effects?"

Troya gives an evasive shrug. "Not really."

Yrin frowns. "What kind of answer is that?"

"Look, are we doing this or not?" Troya asks.

Yrin squeezes his eyes shut and holds out his arm. "Fine, give me the jab."

"Not there," Troya says.

"Where then?" Yrin sees where she's looking. "Oh no, you don't."

"Pants down, Mr Gok," she orders.

A look of horror crosses his face.

"In public?"

"Public. Private. What's the difference? Pants down."

Soon the entire control room is chanting the same instruction.

"Pants down! Pants down!"

"Turn round and look the other way," Yrin snaps, "or I don't do it."

He is bending forward when he dozes off. Troya takes advantage of the moment and jabs the needle into a mighty buttock. Yrin comes to, howling with pain and fury.

"That was sneaky!"

"Oh, stop complaining."

Yrin limps out of the room, rubbing his backside and still grumbling.

"What happened to dignity?" he demands.

Troya waits until he is out of earshot.

"I wonder whether I should have told him about the side effects," she murmurs.

"Why, what are they?"

Troya chuckles. "Extreme flatulence."

"How long will it last?"

"Four, maybe five hours."

For the next few hours nobody goes anywhere near Yrin Gok. The smell is appalling, a combination of rotten eggs, strong cheese and garlic. Every time Yrin breaks wind there is a groan of: "Oh, Yrin" and he stamps out of the room, looking utterly humiliated.

Six hours have passed when he appears at the door. There is a look of triumph on his face.

"The smell has stopped," he announces. "But that's not all."

We look at him expectantly.

"It's worked," he declares. "I haven't dozed off once. The curse is lifted."

"Thank the stars," Troya says. "Now we can roll out the cure to the rest of the Magenti population."

Soon everybody is crowding round Yrin, giving him their heartfelt congratulations. But it is short-lived. Azari's voice interrupts the celebrations.

"There is news from Thren 15," she says. "It's not good."

"Just how bad is it?"

"See for yourself."

She brings up the news broadcast. The presenter is a fire-breathing Meener in military uniform. He is flanked by Skellits, humanoids and a number of Threnassics, all in the same military uniform.

"What the hell....?"

A hush descends over the room, interrupted only by Yrin's gasp of horror.

"Cerberus has done it," he says. "It's a military coup."

Azari turns up the volume.

"The weak and corrupt rule of President Shavlotan is over," the Meener presenter begins, flames licking round his broken, leathery lips. "To save the galaxy from disorder the military junta has taken over the reins of government. Democracy has made us weak. We are not exploiting our resources. We are allowing terrorists to wreck and destroy. The traitor Shavlotan is under arrest. Strong rule will now replace the chaos of the past."

I examine the grainy images, inspecting the personnel in the Presidential Palace's main hall. There, on the far right of the back row, unsmiling, but with eyes alive with triumph, is Liesl Schlachthof.

Eleven

Speed is the keyword. We have to move fast. We enter Thren 15's atmosphere. Already Cerberus will be scrambling their skyflitters to intercept and destroy us. We land in the thickly forested area east of the city.

"Why here?"

Yrin has the answer. "This way we will have some cover. If we landed in the barren west or anywhere within the city boundaries the skyflitters would pick us off before we got anywhere near the Presidential Palace." We shuffle to the doors.

"Move!" Yrin barks, shoving the passengers down the disembarkation ramp. "Move off the open ground. Take cover."

We are travelling light, but we are all armed with our weapons and several doses of the MK antidote in case we encounter any of Yrin's fellow Magenti. Suddenly the word Somnolent is history. It is strange to see Yrin proud, confident, alert....awake. I feel a hand on my arm. It's Azari.

"Quite something, isn't he?" she says.

"I wonder how he felt all that time, you know, being a hero inside and a figure of fun out on the street."

"I think it was tearing him apart," Azari observes. "I've seen his like in my bar, dousing themselves with drink or high on tubes."

I'd seen Hoopwots and Meeners staggering down the street sipping from multi-coloured tubes. So Yrin's people dulled their pain with this stuff too.

By the time we reach the thick, lush, deep purple rainforest, the skyflitters are already on the horizon. Fierce beams of light rake through the foliage. They are searching for any sign of movement.

"Stay down," Yrin orders. "Not a move."

The jungle canopy is so dense that no more than one per cent of the light from Thren 15's twin suns penetrates to the forest floor. I crouch in the dripping gloom, wondering when the assault will begin. I know the score. Cerberus troopers will abseil from their flitters and come looking for us. They will have extermination on their minds. The searchlights continue to rove across the forest, stopping now and then to examine any movement. Twice, startled Thren deer break cover. Twice the searchlights follow them then resume their exploration. Some of the captives we liberated from the Jumeli are getting twitchy.

"Keep your nerve," Yrin tells them. "If they spot us, they will flush us out into the open so they can pick us off from the air. We stand a better chance in a firefight with their troopers."

His calm, quiet authority settles their nerves. So we wait. And wait. The Cerberus commanders are reluctant to deploy their fighters. Their superior firepower will be less effective in close combat in the jungle. Finally, ropes play out from the flitters. The troopers fix their mechanical descenders and start down. Immediately we open fire, taking out at least a dozen while they are hanging defencelessly from their craft. Yrin is running things.

"Pick your target, fire, find cover," he shouts. "Stay where you are and cannon operators on the flitters will pick you off."

One of the survivors of the Jumeli ignores the instruction. I hear the scream. It has cost him his life. By now troopers are falling like ripe fruit and thudding into the forest floor, but they have the numbers. Soon they are fanning out, taking cover and returning fire. Pulse beams cross in the murk and shred the thick foliage. A desperate struggle for survival is beginning. We race through the dripping palm fronds. They are sapphire and ochre, scarlet and emerald. They are like nothing on Earth. Azari holds up three fingers. I squint through the shadows and there they are, three Cerberus troopers creeping round the back of our comrades' position. I see a pulse rifle powering up. The trooper has got Yrin in his crosshairs. I fire. The ZX90 does its job. Azari gestures. Two left.

On Azari's command, I go left. I lose sight of my target. I inch forward, taking care not to make any noise. To my horror I step out right in front of the enemy. They are as surprised and horrified as I am. Nobody reacts. Before I or either of the troopers can recover from our shock and open fire, Azari takes the pair of them down.

"Sorry," I tell her. "I lost them in the bad light."

I am expecting her to yell at me for freezing.

"Forget it," she says. "Anyone would struggle in these conditions. This way."

As we move forward, crouching low, it is hard to know who is friend or who is foe. Shadows shift this way and that. Weapons hum and whine. Screams tear the humid air from time to time. The fighting is chaotic. We step onto a forest path. A huge figure spins round, training his weapon on us.

"Yrin!"

He lowers the rifle.

"You gave me a scare," he says.

He scans the undergrowth.

"They seem to be withdrawing," Yrin tells us. "Yes, look."

We can see two bedraggled columns of Cerberus troopers retreating to a clearing where the flitters can extract them.

"Their commanders are going to evacuate them. We've given them a bloody nose."

But there's a cost. When our people gather after the skirmish there are five dead. Troya is treating the half dozen walking wounded.

"Bury the dead," Yrin says. "We've got to move out before they attack us again."

So there are no eulogies. There is nothing to mark the shallow graves of the fallen. We cover the bodies with soil and move out. For the next few hours everybody is on edge. The flitters glide back and forth, their searchlights skimming the jungle canopy. Finally the lights of the city start to wink through the treetops. Thren 15's twin suns are sinking over the horizon. It is getting dark.

"Get some rest," Yrin orders. "We move into the city in two hours."

We eat silently. I look around. There are a few dozen fighters. It doesn't look much of a liberating army, just a small band of haunted rebels. Yrin wanders round the groups, trying to lift their spirits. Occasionally a flitter hovers overhead before moving on. At last Yrin makes his way over to us.

"Don't tell anybody," he whispers, "but something's wrong."

Troya glances at him. "How so?"

Yrin scratches his head. "I expected them to hit us with everything they've got, cannon fire, lasers, defoliant chemicals. Instead, there's a half-hearted firefight and they withdraw their troops. What gives?"

This is the first time anybody has put it into words, but it is there in everybody's eyes. It has all been too easy. Cerberus is in power on Thren 15, but their attacks are less effective than Don Menchi's back on Metakal.

"So you think they're planning something?"

"I'm sure of it."

I can feel apprehension stealing down my spine. He's right. Cerberus is in charge of a whole planet and here we are walking to the edge of the city with only token opposition. I am still turning it over in my mind when the flitters' speakers crackle to life.

"Rebels," they announce. "We know where you are. We have assessed your firepower."

Azari snorts. "So that's what that skirmish was about. They were counting our guns."

"Deliver the terrorist Henry Kwok to us and your lives will be spared."

"Hear that?" Yrin chuckles. "You're public enemy number one."

"But why me?" I ask. "You're the leader of the rebels, Yrin. Azari is the one who saved the President's life. Why are they so interested in me, a fourteen-year-old kid?"

Yrin frowns. "You're right. It doesn't make any sense."

"Henry was meant to be a fall guy, pretty much a random choice from the humanoids who would survive the wormhole. So why do they still want him?"

Nobody has any answers.

"Hand over Henry Kwok," the speakers repeat, "or we open the gates of Hell."

I stare at Yrin then at Azari and Troya. "Why me?"

Nobody answers. I am aware of everyone staring. Then a scream tips through the gathering darkness and a startled apeling vanishes into the darkness. There is a second shriek of terror and another rebel disappears.

"Skellits!" comes a warning shout. " I saw them. Skell...."

The warning cry ends in a gargling howl of agony.

"Skellits!" Yrin yells, repeating the alert. "It's Skellits. We need light."

"But you said...."

"I know. It could make us targets for the flitters. It's a risk we're going to have to take."

Torches stutter to life. My heart is slamming. I remember the translucent Skellits. All their victims will have seen would have been translucent, protoplasmic forms. Under strong light the Skellits shimmer slightly, making them visible. Here in the woods they are virtually impossible to distinguish. They seem to join with the tree trunks and become part Skellit, part forest.

"I can use the Night Bloom," I say.

"Too dangerous," Azari tells me. "The flitters might miss a few torches. The Night Bloom would be bound to give us away."

There is another scream.

"They're killing us," Troya pants terrified. "We've got to do something."

"Make a circle," Yrin orders. "Face the undergrowth. Keep your weapons directed at the trees."

"Then they'll have us trapped," Azari protests. "They will radio in our position and the flitters will pick us off."

It is Troya who comes up with the solution.

"Those permanganate mushrooms," she says. "Bring them over."

I follow the direction in which she is looking. There is a giant fungus. It is deep purple and it has a radius of at least a metre. I see another. And another.

"What do you want them for?"

"They contain a natural dye. We'll be able to identify the Skellits."

Now I am on her wavelength. Nobody is moving towards the

mushrooms so I take a deep breath and race towards them. I skid on my knees, set the ZX90 to laser cut and start burning through the stem. Yrin joins me. I am almost through when the air shudders in front of me. I can just make out a translucent form looming over me. This time I don't hesitate. I twist the barrel and hit the attacking Skellit with lethal force. While I train my weapon on the dripping blackness, Yrin hauls the mushroom over to Troya. She swings what looks like a bazooka off her back and trains it on the fungus. The weapon is draining fluid from the mushroom.

"Step back!" she yells.

She sprays the forest with the purple liquid. There they are, half a dozen snarling figures. Now they are a bright violet. The dye seems to make them solid. The rebels open fire. Troya repeats the operation, walking round the outside of our defensive circle and soaking the foliage with the dye. Our weapons finish the remaining Skellits, but the danger isn't over. The flitters have got a fix on us. Lethal pulse cannon fire thuds into the forest around us. Suddenly the world is on fire and we're running for our lives. I hear more screams and glance back. Death cries echo in the dark and the mist.

"Keep running!" Yrin yells.

"They're dying."

"There is nothing we can do," Yrin pants. "Our weapons are useless against the flitters. They don't have the range to take craft that size out of the sky. His face is grim, but determined. "Some of us will die. Some will survive. That's the way it is."

I keep on running, but tears are streaming down my face.

Twelve

Some of us die.

Some of us survive.

A few filthy, weary rebels make it into the suburbs of Thren City, haunted by the carnage in the jungle. We gather in one of the shabby projects that sprawl around the periphery of the city. Yrin speaks urgently, his gaze sweeping the high-rise buildings for some sign of attacking flitters.

"We are not an army. We are not a revolution. The people of the city must know we are here."

"And if they don't?"

"If they don't, we die. Cerberus has won."

A flitter appears in the distance. Everybody tenses. It hovers for a moment, searchlights playing across the rows of identical buildings. After a few moments it moves silently on. We relax. Momentarily.

"Azari will lead an attack on the Communication Hub. We need to broadcast an appeal for people to rise up against Cerberus."

"And us?"

"Our target is the Presidential Palace. They are holding Shavlotan there. We need him to unite everybody behind the Republic."

I voice my doubts.

"What if he's already dead?"

Yrin fixes me with a stare. That is something he doesn't want to contemplate.

Azari leads her group into the city. Troya follows.

"Troya's no fighter," I say.

"She can hack into their systems," Yrin tells me.

He turns without another word and leads the way towards the centre of the city, the seat of power and the heart of the new Cerberus dictatorship. Now and then we pause, ducking out of sight to avoid a passing patrol.

"They've been planning this for some time," Yrin grunts. "They had all those starched, new uniforms ready for the big day."

They were prepared all right. I think of Schlachthof, her promises, her lies. I remember the way the flitters called my name. If I was just a random fall guy, why are they so interested in me now? Why am I more important to them than Yrin or Azari? It doesn't make sense.

"Move!" Yrin barks. "Over there."

He pats me on the shoulder. I race across the highway and duck behind a dumpster. A patrol flitter floats by. My heart is kicking in my chest. How are we supposed to bring down Cerberus when it controls the army, the police, the whole apparatus of government?

"Where are we going?" I ask. "The palace is that way."

"We've got something to do first," he answers. "We don't have the numbers to mount a serious assault on the palace. We need reinforcements."

There is a question in my stare.

"Many Magenti are without work," he explains.

I hear the shame in his voice.

"They gather outside the government buildings and wait for them to throw out their leftover food. That's right, they feed it to the Somnolents."

It takes twenty minutes to reach our destination. Concealed beneath the skyways, masked by the gigantic buildings of the government complex, there is a broad square. On this bleak, windswept space hundreds of Magenti are gathered. Yrin strides through the throng. I hear the crimson-haired giants murmuring his name. Some do so and doze off. Yrin springs onto a wall.

"Sisters, brothers," he says, speaking quickly, "for many years we have been treated with contempt. Look at you. You feed on the scraps cast out from the palace. President Shavlotan promised to end our misery. Now he is held captive. If he dies, our hope of freedom dies."

"What can we do?' one of Yrin's listeners demands. "How can we fight back when we....?"

As if to press the point home, he topples forward, fast asleep. His neighbours hold him up and shake him awake.

"I will tell you how we fight back," Yrin replies. "I have stayed awake for eighteen hours at a stretch."

A murmur of disbelief runs through the crowd.

"Do you want to know how I did it?" he asks.

He has the attention of the mass of Magenti. He holds up one of the injection guns.

"Our affliction was no accident. Cerberus did it to break our power. That's right, the aurora was a weapon. This is the antidote. My comrades will pass among you giving you the treatment. There are side effects...."

I remember the flatulence.

"But it is a small price to pay for our freedom."

We have injected about half the crowd when we attract the attention of Cerberus troopers.

"What's going on down there?" one demands. "You've got your food. Disperse. Go on, move you filthy Somnolents."

Enraged by the insult, one of the Magenti tugs at a paving slab and hurls it at the troopers. The Meener who shouted the insult ducks and reaches for his weapon. Before he can open fire, I take him down with the ZX90. His fellow guards are preparing to unleash a deadly cannonade, but already the treated Magenti are surging up towards them. We give covering fire to the advancing rebels and they overwhelm the troopers. Within minutes, sirens are howling across the complex.

"Finish treating the rest," Yrin orders.

The Magenti are climbing the pillars that support the soaring walkways, racing up steps and escalators, surging over walls and buttresses. Some of the troopers laugh in their faces, expecting them to fall asleep in the middle of the assault. It doesn't happen. Soon, the Magenti have overwhelmed the outnumbered palace guards. We are inside the complex.

"That was the easy bit," Yrin announces. "They will counter-attack. We have to be ready for them."

Soon the Magenti and what is left of the rebel fighters who made their way through the jungle are dodging from cover to cover, advancing on the palace.

"Flitters!" comes the cry.

Half a dozen of the craft loom above the rooftops. Pulse cannon open up, blasting holes in the walkways.

"They are ready to destroy the city to stay in power," Yrin observes grimly.

"What chance do we have?"

"Without a rising across the city," he answers. "None."

I glimpse a pulse cannon battery being set up on the palace walls.

"Could that bring down the flitters?" I ask.

Yrin claps me on the shoulder.

"Well spotted, young Kwok. You're right. They've given us a way to even things up."

Without another word he races forward and starts to scramble up the sheer walls to reach the troopers' defensive position. Explosions are bringing down steel and masonry around him.

"Give him covering fire!" I yell.

A chaotic and unequal firefight follows, but Yrin continues his climb as if he doesn't care about his own fate. The Magenti are taking heavy losses from the flitters. The troopers have spotted Yrin. They are hurling shock grenades to dislodge him. Our steady rain of covering fire forces them to hurry their throw. The grenades miss, but a couple of times Yrin slides a metre or two down the wall before recovering his grip.

"Keep going," I urge. "We're depending on you."

Then there he is, clambering over the parapet. First one, then half a dozen troopers are sent hurtling off the walls and slam onto the ground. We watch the parapet for a few seconds then Yrin appears, blasting away at the flitters. One takes a direct hit and crashes into a communication mast, flames spiralling from its engines. Seeing the damage inflicted on their sister ship, the remaining flitters pull back. Yrin swings his pulse cannon round to face the threat of the troopers massing in the palace compound.

"Get up here," he yells. "I need some of you to operate the rest of the guns."

There is no way I can scale the walls like the Magenti so I race to the steps, mounting them two at a time. By the time I reach Yrin's position there are half a dozen fighters operating the pulse cannon. I pant a question.

"How are we doing?"

"Good," Yrin answers, before pointing at the vast square where I witnessed the assassination attempt on President Shavlotan. "But we've got to do better."

The sky is black with flitters. Assault transports are massing in the square, followed by hundreds of troopers. Even more menacing, amid the Skellits, Meeners and Threnassics heading our way armed to the teeth are a dozen androids, each ten metres tall and heavily armed.

"We've got the numbers for a skirmish," Yrin tells me. "Cerberus is ready for a war."

Thirteen

Yrin's gaze travels over the formidable strike force massing before us. He watches for a while then holds out a meaty hand.

"It's been nice knowing you, young Kwok."

"You think it's over, don't you?"

He treats me to a sad smile.

"I *know* it's over." He checks the level in his pulse rifle. "I'm going to make them pay dearly for my death." He turns to his poorly armed, vastly outnumbered supporters. "Brothers, sisters, forgive me for calling you to arms in a fight we could not win. If only...."

He doesn't get to finish his speech. Music blares out, drowning his words. I recognise it. It's the Presidential anthem, now an illegal demonstration of support for the deposed and imprisoned Shavlotan. Yrin meets my stare.

"You don't think..."

Then there is the unmistakable sound of Azari's voice.

"Citizens," she cries, her voice singing out across the city. "Whether you be Skellit or Threnassic, Hoopwot or apeling, humanoid or Meener, you have been betrayed. The Cerberus conspiracy has seized power in an illegal coup. President Shavlotan speaks for all. Rise up. Free our elected leader."

Silence follows. I see the troopers looking at each other, uncertain how to react.

"They're hesitating."

"I wouldn't expect too much," Yrin tells me. "The troopers may have some sympathy for Shavlotan, but soldiers obey orders."

"Look up at the screens," Azari continues.

An image flashes up. It shows a pulse rifle being pointed at President Shavlotan's head.

"Is this the rule of law?" Azari demands. She is warming to her theme. "Will you serve a conspiracy that would kill our president?"

There are shouts of no, mostly from the Magenti behind us. But there are a few from the troopers.

"Still think they'll obey orders?" I ask.

"That was the President half an hour ago," Azari cries.

This time the screen shows film of Azari and Troya leading a rebel force into the cell where the President was being held.

"But how?'

"Clever girl," Yrin chuckles. "While Cerberus threw everything against us, she worked her way round the back of the compound and liberated the President."

The film of the President's rescue ends. In its place there is the President himself, seated at his desk. Some of the troopers twist round to look at the palace.

"Citizens, soldiers," the President begins. "The Cerberus gangsters have plotted my downfall for many years. Cerberus does not want a Republic governed by its own people. It wants the rule of the few, the slavery of the many. "

One of the troopers' commanders tries to shoot out the screens, but his soldiers overwhelm him.

"Let the President speak," some of them shout to applause.

The mood is changing fast. The troopers have almost forgotten about us.

"Rise up against your commanders," Shavlotan cries. "Take away their arms. They serve Cerberus, not the leader you voted to install as President."

The troopers seize their officers' arms.

"We will fight for our Republic," Shavlotan thunders. "We will fight for the citizens' voice to be heard. For freedom!"

The troopers raise their weapons above their heads.

"For freedom!" they roar.

For a few moments there is elation then there is a reminder of Cerberus' power. A familiar face appears at an upper window of the palace.

"Liesl Schlachthof!"

She has something in her hand. For a moment I am puzzled by her actions. She is looking at something and pressing a kind of remote control. I turn. My blood runs cold.

"The androids," I shout. "She's activating the androids."

As if to confirm my warning one of the giants opens fire on the troopers. They stream across the walkways and squares, trying to find cover. Some make it. Others die where they were standing. Flames boil across the square. Dense, choking smoke swirls around us. The androids come remorselessly forward, lethal power roaring forth. The rebels return fire, but ineffectually. There are no weapons on the rebel side that can do any damage to these monsters. Each time the androids use their weapons the squares and walkways before them transform into an inferno. If we don't stop them it is over.

I put my thoughts into words. "There has to be a way to bring them down."

Yrin glances at me. "If we had cables we could topple them. We don't."

"We've got to do something."

Yrin shakes his head. "There is nothing we can do. We have to withdraw."

"Then Cerberus has won."

Yrin shrugs. "If we stay here we die."

Then something happens that changes the balance of forces. A blurry shape rushes through the firestorm and climbs the nearest android. A huge, spiky limb smashes into its head, tearing out the control system. The shadowy form springs across to the next android, swinging it round physically to use it to open fire on the other machines.

"It can't be," I gasp. "He's dead."

But there is no mistaking the Arachnibrid. Within a matter of minutes the androids are disabled and the rebels are surging forward again, disarming the few troopers who are still loyal to Cerberus.

"Let's find Azari, Troya...and the President," Yrin roars.

We see the Arachnibrid lumbering towards us.

"We thought you were dead."

"So did I. I keep courting death, but it refuses my approaches."

"How did you get here?"

"I paid Don Menchi a visit. He loaned me his spaceship."

Yrin grins. "Out of the goodness of his heart?"

The Arachnibrid's eight eyes sparkle. "There may have been a little gentle persuasion."

"Welcome back, brother," Yrin says. "It's time to end the threat of the Cerberus conspiracy."

Already the rebels are streaming through the doors of the Presidential Palace, flushing troopers loyal to Cerberus out of the side rooms. There is still no sign of Azari, Troya or President Shavlotan. I follow Yrin up an escalator. Then there is movement. I glimpse it out of the corner of my eye and spin round. To my relief a familiar face fills my sight.

"Azari."

"Follow me," she says. "There is somebody I want you to meet...and something you need to see, Henry."

There is something in her voice that makes my heart pound with apprehension.

Fourteen

"It's not possible!"

"Why not?"

"James Wong. My friend James Wong, He winds up President of the USA! It doesn't make any sense. I mean, he's fourteen."

"You've got to look at the big picture, Henry," President Shavlotan tells me. "People grow up. The James of your childhood grows up to be one of the most powerful men in the world."

"How? He was the class loner until I befriended him."

"People change."

Troya brings up a screen.

"Here's the proof if you don't believe us. He becomes President of the USA thirty years after you disappear. This is the history on Liesl Schlachthof's computer. Look for yourself."

She pulls up the files. Each time a clip plays. I watch my friend's life unfold before me: the return to San Francisco when he is sixteen, his involvement in university politics, his days as a human rights lawyer, a Congressman at thirty-five, President in his early forties."

"But how did you make the connection, Troya? How did you know there was a link between me and James?"

Troya glances at Azari. She takes over.

"We didn't," she tells me. "We were searching Schlachthof's recent history to see if it would help us track her down. We came across this."

In the clip James is in his late thirties, a Congressman on the West Coast. He is making an appeal for a missing teenager. His words cut me to the core:

"I know the pain of such a loss. When I was fourteen my best friend, a boy called Henry Kwok, vanished. It almost destroyed his family. He went to bed one night and in the morning he was gone. Nobody ever saw him again."

There is somebody next to him.

"Anna!"

She holds up a photo.

"This is Anna's brother Henry as he was." I stare at the photo of me. Then James produces a second one. "This is Toni Nelson. She has vanished just as Henry did. We lost Henry forever. He was a good friend, a loved brother and son. You can help return Toni to her folks. If you have seen her or if you know anything about her whereabouts, call this number."

A number runs along the bottom of the screen, but I can't read it. Tears are blurring my vision. It's a while before I can speak. To see my best friend and my sister standing side by side, thirty years older, talking about me as if I'm dead, is the strangest feeling of my life. I swallow hard, struggling to stem the flow of tears.

"Are you OK, Henry?" Azari asks.

I shake my head.

"What does this mean?"

Azari continues pulling up the files. I watch the talking heads, the racing images.

"Stop!" I yell suddenly. "Go back."

"Did you see something?" Troya asks.

See is the wrong word. Something leapt out at me and grabbed my attention.

"I don't know. Yes, there."

It's a confirmation email for a hotel booking in London, dated thirty years after I left home, the same year James becomes President. There is a familiar face on a scanned passport page. It is in the name of Lisa Stanton, but the initials are the same. LS.

"Liesl Schlachthof."

"It's her," Troya agrees. "She has gone back to your home planet. But why?"

136

"There is only one reason," Yrin says.

I stare at him. "Which is?"

"Think about it, Henry. Remember what you told us. You weren't convinced by her story. There had to be something more to it. This is it. Liesl Schlachthof can travel through time. She must have known about your friend."

I search my memory.

"It's possible," I murmur. "He said he had something to tell me the last time I saw him, but I was too busy with everything that was happening to me. Why didn't I listen?"

"James becomes the new President of the United States. It's the same story. Cerberus has failed here. It is going to strike there."

Yrin's right. Of course he's right. That's how Liesl Schlachthof came to choose me. I wasn't special. James was. He was the future President, somebody she could influence, somebody she could manipulate.

"I was just a handy fall guy. I was an accident."

"So don't be an accident."

I hear the voice and turn round. It is President Shavlotan.

"We are interrogating a number of captured Cerberus agents. Liesl Schlachthof is one of the organisation's key researchers and strategists. Maybe she had plans for your friend James then put them on ice when she saw a chance to assassinate me and take power here. We have no way of knowing. Cerberus is broken in this time, this place. You must break them in your time and your home, Henry Kwok, or it all starts over. You must go back."

"But how can I go back?"

President Shavlotan glances at the others then leads the way down a long corridor.

"In there," he says.

"But it's a service room."

"You'll find what you're looking for."

I open the door. There are ducts, pipes, dials, digital panels. This is where they control the lights and heating of the whole building.

"Here?"

"Go to your left."

I do as he says. I walk. President Shavlotan follows. Azari, Troya, Yrin and the Arachnibrid wait by the door. What is this?

"There is a recess," the president tells me. "That's where you will find it."

My companions have now arrived behind him.

"What's the big deal?" I demand. "Why are you being so secretive?"

Azari is the one who answers. "We thought you should see for yourself."

I peer into the recess. Now I understand. There is an open pyramid erected on a base of three circular metal discs. It is identical to the time machine that brought me here.

"She's already gone back!"

"That's right, Henry. We disturbed her. She had set a timer to destroy this time terminal. She escaped, but we prevented her closing this gateway. You must follow her."

"Now?"

Troya gives the apeling equivalent of a smile.

"Not now. We have to make preparations for your departure. She is an experienced and dangerous operator. We have to even things up."

I interrupt her. "This is all going too fast. What am I supposed to do when I get back?"

President Shavlotan seems taken aback by the question.

"Why, you've got to stop them."

I'm getting frustrated. "Stop who...from doing what?"

"You mean you don't know? You are unaware of your own planet's history?"

"I don't..."

"You know that some of Earth's population took to their space cruisers in search of new worlds?"

"Yes. Liesl Schlachthof told me."

"But you don't know why?"

"Earth's resources were exhausted."

"That's part of it," President Shavlotan agrees, "but there were plans to mine asteroids for minerals. There was no need to leave Earth. Star travel wasn't the first option on the agenda or the easiest."

"So what changed?"

"It seems Ms Schlachthof left out the most important reason for abandoning Earth when she related the planet's history."

"So what was the reason?"

"The bomb, Henry. Your friend James presses the red button. He launches the nuclear war that kills most of the planet's population."

I stare in horror.

"Cerberus' founders left Earth on those first transports. Without the war Cerberus would never have crossed the starways, would never have set up an organisation that could topple governments, would never have brought the universe within a hair's breadth of total war. That's what she wanted your friend for, Henry. Together, they will destroy your planet."

Fifteen

It is twenty-four hours before I am ready to go.

Troya has worked without a break on the equipment to give me a fighting chance against Liesl Schlachthof.

"This phone will instantly hack into any computer system you wish to access," she explains. "The firewalls in the mid twenty-first century were pathetically weak. You will be able to pay hotel and restaurant bills, take out cash, discover the password to any computer. You will also be able to hack into communication systems, public utilities, security networks."

"A phone can do all that?"

"I'll show you. But first, you have to see this."

She holds a translucent capsule between her thumb and forefinger.

"What is it?"

"Skellit extract."

"Come again?"

"When the Skellits attacked us in the forest, I extracted some of their DNA. This tablet can give you their unique ability to become virtually invisible for twenty, maybe thirty minutes."

"They're not just invisible though, are they?"

"No. Few understand how their bodies work. Maybe this extract will give you a clue."

"Half an hour isn't long. Why can't I just take a bigger dose?"

"Not wise," Troya says. "It would dissolve your spine and poison your central nervous system. The Skellits know how to live with their condition. You don't."

I nod. "Taking too much doesn't sound wise at all."

"Let's get to work," she says. "You need to be proficient with all the equipment."

The training takes less than an hour.

"The ZX90 will be no good to you where you're going," she says. "You need a weapon that can be easily concealed about your person." She holds up a mobile phone. "You can't make calls, but you can do this."

She spins round and reduces a door to dust. Yrin shakes his head.

"Now the lab needs a new door."

Troya chuckles. "Maybe I should have thought about it before I did the demonstration." Her face becomes serious. "One last thing," she says. "The phone has a second feature. You must only use it in desperate circumstances."

She thumbs the screen across to a new setting.

"What does it do?" I ask.

"It will make you weightless for twenty, maybe thirty seconds. After that you will fall like a stone. If you have to use it, choose the location very carefully indeed."

I stare at the kit.

"But what use is all this stuff? I can't take it with me. I couldn't even wear clothes or a belt."

Troya taps her virtual keyboard and a film starts to run in front of us.

"These are the surveillance recordings for the service room. Watch."

Liesl Schlachthof loads some equipment into a box and shoves it into the time pyramid. It vanishes. A moment later, she wriggles into the space and follows it.

"So she has developed a way of sending objects through space and time."

"Our Ms Schlachthof is nothing if not inventive," Troya observes. "I ran a scan and duplicated the box. You can do exactly the same."

"Clothes?"

"In the box."

"So I'm ready?"

Yrin rests a huge hand on my shoulder, calming, reassuring. "Only you can know that, young Kwok."

"My world needs me to be ready," I answer. "So I will be."

Azari likes that. "Sounds remarkably like wisdom, Henry."

I shake my head. "It's been a long while coming. I swallowed every stupid lie Liesl Schlachthof invented. No matter how insane the stories she was weaving I swallowed them whole. How could I be so stupid?"

Yrin seems to find my lousy mood amusing. "You make it sound as if we have lost, young Kwok. Cerberus is on the run. The President is back in power. The peace conference can go ahead."

"And Liesl Schlachthof has gone back in time to undo our victory. On the way she is going to blow up my planet. My mum and dad are there, Yrin, and my sister."

So I do care about Anna!

Troya breaks in on my thoughts. "It's time to go, Henry. The coordinates are set. We have a window of ten minutes."

She puts the box containing my clothes into the pyramid. I watch the pulsating sapphire light until the box vanishes.

"Your turn, Henry."

Everybody is watching me.

"What are you doing? Turn your backs. I've got to strip to my underwear."

"Oh!"

They all turn. That's how we say our goodbyes, me stripping to my boxer shorts, them staring at a blank wall. I scramble into the pyramid.

"I'll miss you guys."

"We'll miss you, Henry Kwok."

I activate the pyramid. By the time they turn round I will be gone.

Story three: The third head of Cerberus

One

I stare at the city scene. It is more futuristic than the world I left, but there is only one sun, no flitters roam the skies, no aliens walk the streets. It is Earth, but not as I know it. This is Piccadilly, at the heart of London's West End. It looks familiar. The shell of picture postcard London is intact. In a way, I am disappointed that there has been so little change in thirty years. There are the iconic, bright red Routemaster buses gliding down the street, but there is something different about them. They are silent. A battery must power the engine, probably similar to the nickel-metal hydride batteries they used in the first generation of hybrid vehicles. The buses are the only vehicles visible. The streets are otherwise pedestrianised. A monorail zips silently across the sky. I cross the road to the Ritz hotel and approach the desk. The receptionist treats me to an indifferent stare.

"Yes?"

"Can you tell me which room Liesl....Lisa Stanton is in?"

"We don't divulge guests' details," he tells me.

"Fine, so can you call her room for me?"

He taps some details into his computer. It is already the keyboard-free technology I encountered in the distant future.

"Miss Stanton has booked a room," he informs me, "but she hasn't checked in yet."

"OK. Could I have my key please?" I read his lapel badge. "Ricardo."

He looks surprised that I am a guest at the hotel. He returns to his computer.

"Name?"

"Kwok. Henry Kwok."

I booked the reservation earlier with the card Troya made me.

"Are your parents not with you?" he asks.

"No," I tell him, delivering my well-rehearsed cover story. "Our flight was delayed. They had to go straight to a function."

The receptionist is uncertain.

"How old are you, sir?"

"Fourteen," I tell him. "Old enough to cross London by myself."

"We don't usually issue room keys to a minor without their parents being present."

"These are unusual circumstances," I remind him. "My parents won't be happy if I am left hanging round the foyer for two hours. They will have to contact the Embassy."

Nice touch, if I say so myself. Ricardo calls his line manager over. They whisper for a moment.

"I will issue your key card," he says. "I will need the swipe of a credit card when they arrive."

"Dad gave me his card," I tell him, placing it on the desk.

Troya thought of everything.

Ricardo stares. "Your father trusts you with his credit card?"

"He does. I am very trustworthy."

I say it as confidently as I can. Ricardo has another heads-together with his boss and swipes the card. He hands me a printed authorisation and the key card.

"Do you have any luggage?" he asks.

I shake my head. "My parents take care of all that stuff."

"Of course."

Before he can get somebody to show me to my room I snatch the key card from the desk, register the number and head for the lifts. My room is plush. The colour scheme is gold and cream. I flop on the bed, hands laced behind my head and stare at the ceiling.

"You did good, young Kwok," I tell myself, echoing Yrin.

I gaze at the ceiling for maybe two minutes then I realise I am hungry. I order room service: seabass with langoustine, coco beans and basil. It arrives twenty minutes later and I eat at the circular table by the window.

"OK, Liesl, Lisa, whatever you're calling yourself, let's see if you've arrived yet," I say out loud.

I set the mobile phone Troya gave me to internet function and hack into the hotel computer. Lisa, I mean Liesl, still hasn't checked in.

"I can wait."

I wait all afternoon. I wait all evening. There is no sign of her so I stand at the window and look at the city. I imagine every electric light turned into a flame, every building transformed into rubble. It is a long time before I can get to sleep.

I wake about six and use the mobile to check the hotel's records. Lisa Stanton has still not checked in. OK, there is something wrong. Why would she make a reservation for at a London hotel and not turn up? I turn on the TV and there's the answer staring me in the face. It is right there on the screen.

Breaking news.

Middle Eastern crisis deepens.

China and Russia threaten retaliation if US puts troops on the ground.

President Wong under pressure to act.

I feel so stupid. Liesl wanted us to see that passport page. I find myself wondering if you have to give your passport ID to a hotel at all. I was so keen to put things right I jumped at the first sign of a clue. Oh, you're good Ms Schlachthof, you're really good! The action isn't going to happen here in London. It never was. The President is in Washington. That's where he will hit the nuclear button.

I use the mobile to book a flight to Washington. OK, I can make the 10:10 flight. It takes six hours and twelve minutes. London is five hours ahead of Washington so I will land at 11:05. Six hours. It was eight hours back in my own time. They've made progress, but not as much as you'd expect. Maybe the future is not all it's cracked up to be. I think of Yrin and Azari, Troya and the Arachnibrid, different in many ways but all too similar in others. I think about the time it will take to get to Washington. I just hope we still have a world worth living in by the time I arrive. I pick up the phone.

"Yes?"

It's Ricardo.

"This is Henry Kwok in room 336. I'm going to Heathrow. Can you book me a taxi for seven?"

There is a moment's hesitation.

"A taxi?"

"Yes. Why, what's wrong with that?"

"You haven't visited London very often, have you? A taxi would take at least five hours."

"The traffic doesn't look that bad," I protest.

"That is in the Congestion Zone. The rest of the city is gridlocked. You will have to take the monorail."

"Fine."

I take a shower and go for breakfast. I start with cereal and orange juice. Then it is two fried eggs, served with back bacon, Cumberland sausage, black pudding, grilled mushrooms, toast and tea. I go to catch the monorail. The last thing I see is a confused-looking Ricardo wondering where the elusive Mr and Mrs Kwok have got to now.

TWO

With no luggage to slow me down, I expect to get through Washington Dulles airport in minutes. As it turns out there's a two-hour queue for security checks. Anybody with the faintest resemblance to somebody from the Middle East is interrogated. Some are guided to an interview room. I learn from a brief surf of the Net that there have been numerous foiled bombings of the US, including two assassination attempts on President James Wong and his Vice President Maria Chavez. One took place when he was visiting a school in Texas. The other was during a press conference at Chicago's new Obama airport.

Finally, I get through security and jog to the shuttle. This isn't a bus, but a monorail system similar to the one in London. As we speed over Washington's urban sprawl I see the reason for the growth in monorail. Every road is jammed. The urban transport system has been turned into a choking, crawling hell.

I book into the Willard Intercontinental. I am getting used to the luxury lifestyle. The receptionist frowns when I reel off my story about my parents being late.

"Is your name Ricardo?" I ask.

That earns me a frown.

"No, my name is Ignacio."

"Can you hurry it up with my key, please? Things usually go a bit more smoothly than this. Do you want me to phone Dad at the Embassy?"

At the mention of the magic word Embassy, Ignacio does a Ricardo and speeds up the process of checking me in. I march triumphantly to the lift. On the way up I become aware of the other guests' sidelong looks. One smartly dressed woman actually sniffs. Is she smelling me? I suppose I can't blame her. I have been in the same clothes for days. They are crumpled and probably a touch wiffy. Once I've had a look round my room I go out on a shopping expedition. After each purchase I pause to scroll through the news. President Wong is addressing the UN. He will be back at the White House this evening. So what's Liesl's plan? I try to second-guess her. She isn't trying to assassinate James the way she was trying to take out President Shavlotan. She needs him alive so he can press the red button and unleash nuclear Armageddon. So she needs to get close to James. How's she going to do that? Pretty soon my eyelids are drooping. The flight has taken it out of me. I drop onto the bed and fall fast asleep. I wake up an hour, two hours later to the sound of CNN. I lie half asleep on the bed for a few moments then the feature has me sitting up, eyes glued to the screen.

"Is romance in the air? Opponents of President James Wong say that public sympathy after the death of his first wife Caroline was one of the factors propelling him into office. Now it looks like the President has a new love, gorgeous intern Lisa Stanton."

I stare at the familiar blond features. Haven't you been busy, Liesl? She must have been travelling back and forth through time. Impressive.

"The relationship has caused some White House observers to raise their eyebrows. Little is known about the mysterious Miss Stanton. The team here at CNN is doing some digging. Watch this space. Lyle?"

Anchor Lyle Braxton thanks the reporter and introduces an analysis of the worsening Middle East crisis. I am only half listening. Liesl fills my thoughts. I remember the way she sweet-talked me. Now she's got James falling at her feet. Problem is, the only button I had my finger on was the microwave. He has access to an arsenal of destructive power that will reduce the Earth to a cinder.

OK, a plan, I need a plan, only I don't have one. How is a fourteen-year-old kid meant to thwart a criminal mastermind's conspiracy to blow up the world? Where's Spiderman when you need him? I find myself sliding into depression. This is all too much. I jumped at it when President Shavlotan suggested I go back in time and save the world. It was the Liesl factor all over again. When you've got a guiding spirit you feel like you can do anything. Then you're alone again, alone, vulnerable, afraid. I lay out the things Troya gave me: the phone, the capsule. There's something else. I hadn't noticed it, a small black cube. I sit examining, wondering what it is. Troya didn't mention it. Suddenly it unfolds and forms a small screen. A film clip starts to run. Yrin's face appears.

"If you're watching this, it means you have reached your destination safely. We thought you might be feeling alone and in need of a friendly face."

Tears well up as I watch and listen.

"Go for it, Henry. You must know by now that Liesl has wheedled her way into the White House. She is manipulating the President, pushing him ever closer to a disastrous war. Be strong, Henry Kwok. This is your destiny."

Azari, Troya and the Arachnibrid join him.

"We are always with you, Henry."

I brush away the tears and shove everything in my pocket. The President's entourage should be back at the White House soon. It is time to go. I cross the city by taxi. Everything Ricardo said of London is equally true of Washington. The traffic crawls through strangled streets 24/7. The planet's swollen population is making ordinary life impossible. The news bulletins are full of two issues. One is the Middle East crisis. The other is the problem of over population. There are constant demonstrations calling for star travel as an alternative to the chaos on Earth. When we have failed to move for ten minutes I tell the taxi driver I will make the rest of the way on foot. I pay the fare and walk through the darkening streets. What's the plan? Get to the Oval Office, hope James and Liesl are there, challenge her to come clean. OK, it isn't the greatest plan, but it beats sitting in a hotel room feeling sorry for myself. The walk takes ten minutes. I turn a corner and there it is, one of the most famous buildings in the world.

1600 Pennsylvania Avenue.

The White House.

Three

I roam the perimeter of the White House complex. Soldiers in uniform and plain clothes security service operatives move across the manicured lawns. The barking of dogs fills the evening air. Here and there torches bob in the gathering gloom. There is no way I am just going to walk through the door. I didn't expect to. I find myself rolling the capsule of Skellit extract round on my palm. I remember the creepy feeling I always get when the creatures are anywhere near. Do I really want to become like them? The thought makes me shiver. My presence attracts the attention of a couple of security types.

"Move on, son," the younger guy tells me. "There's nothing to see here."

Hey, they really do say it. I thought that was something you only got to hear in the movies.

The older man frowns. "Bit late to be out for a boy your age, isn't it?"

I shrug. "My dad's waiting in the car."

"I don't see him."

"He's having a smoke."

The younger guy smiles. "Tell him it's bad for his health."

"I do. All the time."

When they're gone I come to a decision and pop the capsule in my mouth. At first nothing happens. Then I get the strangest sensation. My skin is as cold as river water when you break the ice. The chill works through me like some glacial energy, working into the marrow of my bones, my veins, my flesh. Somehow, it isn't unpleasant. I feel kind of dreamy, as if I am lying half asleep in bed, but my dream-self is still there with me. That's how it is with the cold. It is part of me, yet something apart. That's when I glimpse my arm. It is barely there. If I didn't look hard I wouldn't be able to distinguish the outline of my body.

"Cool."

I reach for the railings, but instead of grasping them my hands slip through. There is just the suspicion of a gluey, sucking sound. I try the trick with my body. In a matter of seconds I have allowed the bars to pass through me. There is no pain, just the sense of something shuddering inside my stomach and chest. I am starting to understand how the Skellits' bodies work. They are composed of a kind of dense, frozen jelly, not quite cold enough to become solid and brittle. It allows them to pass through some objects and mould themselves into others. They are never quite invisible, but they can be hard to distinguish from the background against which they stand.

I move silently through the grounds, pausing by the bushes and trees whenever the security personnel walk by. Strangely, the dogs don't register my presence. That must be another quality the Skellits have.

They are completely odourless. Before long I am crossing the North Lawn. I notice an ancient elm to my left in its pale yellow autumn foliage. I pause by the fountain. If only I had some way of locating Liesl. How long have I been walking through the grounds? I guess three or four minutes at most. That gives me twenty, twenty-five minutes to thwart Liesl's plan. How the hell do I do that? Once more, I feel out of my depth.

In the end, a kind of inertia carries me forward. I slip in behind some security guards and pad quietly behind them. One spins round and points his weapon straight at me. My heart pounds, but he looks right through me.

"Something wrong, Matt?"

Matt gives a long look then shakes his head.

"Must be this stuff in the Middle East. It's got me spooked."

Having a gun pointed right at me didn't do me much good either!

They flash their passes at a pad on the wall and enter the main building. I follow them inside. They turn left down a corridor. I go right. OK, I'm inside. Now what? There are people speaking everywhere. I strain to distinguish those of James or Liesl among the disembodied, echoing voices. I reach the West Wing. I recognise it from TV. Those doors, they lead to the Oval Office. There is a buzz of conversation inside. I try to work out the chances of James and Liesl being in there. Do I just walk in or could I trigger some kind of alarm. In the event, I wait patiently until a member of the White House staff comes hurrying down the corridor and throws open the door. I follow her inside.

"Mr President!" she cries. "The emergency just got a whole lot worse. They are training their missiles on Israel. This could be it."

My gaze travels across the room. It's James, my old friend, a few decades older, but recognisable as the same guy I hung out with. James curses. He didn't do that when I knew him, at least not when his parents were around.

"I feel like piggy in the middle," he hisses. "Every time I get one side to stand down, the other ups the ante. Why the hell did I take this job?"

"I haven't finished, Mr President. China has issued an ultimatum. If the US fleet doesn't withdraw immediately she will consider our nations at war."

A groan of dismay rumbles round the room.

"China needs our answer, Mr President."

"How long do I have?"

"An hour, sir."

James slumps forward, head heavy, shoulders bowed by the weight of responsibility.

"Give me ten minutes, people. I need to think."

The instruction clears the Oval Office in a matter of minutes. I am still wondering whether I should announce my presence when the door opens and in walks Liesl Schlachthof. She looks stunning in a scarlet dress, but she would look amazing in a cardboard box.

"I heard, James."

"They're playing hardball, Lisa."

"You can't back down. This country has been backing off for decades. It's time we showed we're still Number One."

"Honey, I could push the world into nuclear catastrophe."

"They'll back down. You know they will."

She wanders behind him and starts massaging his shoulders. That's when I notice something in her palm. What is it? I edge forward, craning to look. I can see a small, circular device. There are a couple of sharp prongs. Suddenly I understand. If she can't convince James then she is going to drive this thing into his neck and take control of his mind. Her eyes narrow and she draws back her hand.

"Look out, James!"

Simultaneously, James leaps out of his seat and Liesl's hand slips. Her momentum carries her forward and she buries the device into the desk.

"Who said that?"

"It's me, James. Henry. Henry Kwok."

Liesl tugs at the device, hoping James hasn't noticed it embedded in the desk. At the sound of my voice her eyes widen in astonishment. It gives me a good feeling.

"Where are you?"

"Here. Right here."

Even as the words leave my lips the door bursts open. Security staff pour in.

"We heard a crash, Mr President. Is everything OK?"

"There's an intruder."

Weapons slip from holsters. Gun barrels sweep the room.

"There's nobody here."

"I heard a voice."

That's when the capsule finally wears off. Security men pile on top of me and I am kissing the floor.

"Let me up!" I cry. "I'm not the danger. She is. Look at the desk. Examine that object. Tell me it isn't suspicious."

They don't let me go, but at last James has seen the mind control device.

"What is this, Lisa?"

When there is no answer, he instructs her to sit down.

"Watch her," he says grimly. "I need to know what's going on here."

He turns and examines me. I see recognition light his features.

"Henry. Dear God, Henry, it is you. But how...? You haven't aged a day."

"There's no time to explain now," I tell him. "You have to put her under arrest. She is a terrorist. She means to provoke nuclear war."

That is the signal for Liesl to act. She slides a ring from her finger and tosses it to the floor. Instantly, a shock wave roars across the room. A booming sound fills my head. By the time the impact fades, Liesl has gone.

"Go after her!" James yells.

In the confusion I am out of the door first and onto the lawn. There is movement in the shadows.

"There!"

I take a risk and use the weightlessness mode on the phone. I hurtle through the air and crash on top of Liesl. We struggle for a few moments then I start to choke. She has sprayed me with something. My eyes sting. My throat tightens. It feels like my face is on fire. By the time my vision clears she is vanishing into the distance. I race down the pavement after her. Sirens echo across the city. A helicopter has scrambled and searchlights sweep the streets. Where the hell is she? I have the phone in my hand ready to fire. I catch the sound of running footsteps. Where? Then I spot her racing up the steps of the Washington Monorail. She flashes a pass at the barrier. I vault over it.

We're on the platform, Liesl just metres ahead of me. There is a monorail in the station. She makes it through the doors just as they close. I follow. The doors close on me for a moment then spring back. It has only held me up for a moment, but it has given her a lead.

She has reached the next carriage. I am still struggling with the door when she fires. The shock wave throws me onto my back. Passengers start screaming. I manage to get to my feet, still dazed and groggy, when there is a second blast and a rush of air. At the second attempt, I make it into the carriage.

"Where is she?" I yell.

A woman points.

"She blew out that window."

I rush to the shattered window and look outside. The rushing wind stings my eyes. Liesl has a weightlessness mode on her phone just like the one Troya designed for me. I've used the application. There is only one thing for it. As she launches herself into the air, I propel myself forward and cling to her.

"Are you crazy?" she yells.

We hurtle into the sky, but not in the controlled way Liesl was expecting. We are spinning and twisting, cutting a crazy, irregular path through the night.

"Let go!" she screams. "You're going to get us both killed."

"You should have thought of that when you decided to blow up the world."

"I was doing it to free mankind of this useless chunk of rock. We can't fulfil our potential if we cling to planet Earth."

"You're insane, you know that?"

Finally we hit the ground. Luckily we have come down in a park and we are cutting a channel through the manicured lawns. We come to a halt in a tangled heap. There was a time when I would have dreamed of being this close to her. Now I could only think of one thing: how do I draw my weapon before she uses hers. I fumble for the phone then a searing pain screams through my hand. She has got to her feet first and stamped on my wrist. I see her towering over me. She points her phone at me.

"At point blank range this will fuse your eyelids to your forehead and blast a hole as big as a baseball through your idiot face," she yells.

"And there was me thinking you were a lady!"

She points the weapon. I close my eyes and swallow hard. But the final explosion doesn't come. When I reopen my eyes I see an unconscious Liesl Schlachthoff dangling in the air at the end of a familiar spiky leg.

"It's you."

The Arachnibrid's eight eyes flash.

"But how?" I ask.

"Troya worked non-stop to find a way to send one of us through time to help you. Some nonsense about bio-rhythms."

"So you knew Liesl would get the better of me."

The Arachnibrid grunts.

"Liesl Schlachthof is a match for any man. Don't feel bad."

Strangely, I don't.

"What happens now?"

"I take her back," the Arachnibrid says.

"And me?"

"That's your choice."

"I don't understand."

"The pyramid portal will be open three days from now between eight and nine o'clock in the evening. You have unfinished business here on Earth. If you want to stay, we understand. If you decide to come back to Thren 15 we will be waiting for you. Cerberus is fighting back. We could do with your help."

I hear a helicopter approaching.

"That is the President's security staff," the Arachnibrid murmurs. "I've got to go."

As he scurries away into the distance I turn to see the helicopter landing. As the draught of the rotor blades whips my face I wonder what happens next.

Four

The press conference draws to a close.

"Will this be a lasting peace, Mr President?"

James' gaze settles on the reporter from The New York Times.

"I spoke to the Chinese President this morning. He is as determined as I am to settle this crisis through diplomatic channels."

He leaves the podium and comes backstage.

"How did I do, Henry?"

"You sounded just like President Shavlotan."

"I beg your pardon?"

"Oh, my weird sense of humour."

"It's strange seeing you no older. How could this have happened?"

I stick to my story that I have no recollection of the last thirty years. It's going to save me a whole load of interrogation.

"Walk with me."

We wander across the White House lawn.

"I allowed Lisa to influence my decisions. I regret that now."

"You didn't allow her to control you," I remind him. "That's why she had to resort to using that device."

"The research institute is still trying to analyse it," James tells me. "They say the technology is way beyond anything we know."

"Strange that," I say.

I can feel his eyes on me.

"Why do I get this feeling you know more than you're letting on?"

I give a shrug of the shoulders.

"Beats me," I say, "because I don't."

James doesn't believe me, but I don't press it.

"You didn't recognise Liesl as the woman you met when you were a kid?"
I ask.

"She was familiar, but how could somebody reappear thirty years later
without ageing? I thought it was somebody who bore an uncanny
resemblance to the woman who came into my life all those years ago.
You've got to remember, I only met Liesl the one time when I was a kid.
I wonder what happened to her."

I look away. He doesn't need to know. Besides, how would I explain that
she is in a top security prison two hundred years in the future and half
a universe away?

"The car will be here soon. Are you ready for this?"

I drop my voice. "I don't know. Meeting Mum and Dad after all these
years. Seeing Anna."

"It will be emotional."

"Yes."

But will it? Do I want it to be? I'm not the same kid who left Hong Kong.
Can I really just walk back into their lives and pick up where I left off?

"You don't sound as if you're looking forward to it."

"Oh, it's not that. It might be a bit strained, that's all."

"You'll get over it."

"Sure. Yes, you're right."

The car picks me up five minutes later. James waves me off and I gaze at
the crowded streets as we weave through the mid-morning traffic. We
finally pull up at a downtown hotel. I make my way into the lobby and
freeze.

"Henry!"

It's Mum. She hurtles towards me. She seems smaller somehow. She throws her arms around me. I barely recognise her. She is an old lady now. Dad is grey-haired and stoops as he walks. After the embraces, Anna comes over.

"This is a miracle," she says. "I made an appeal for a kid like you."

"I know," I tell her. "I saw the film."

We have lunch. They ask all kinds of questions. I stick to the amnesia story. They return to the puzzle again and again. How can a kid vanish for thirty years and come back exactly the same age? Anna jokes that I must have been a victim of alien abduction. She is closer to the truth than she knows.

"We've prepared a room for you," Mum says. "Of course, it won't be the same. We live in New York now."

"I retire in a few months," Dad tells me. "Maybe we can spend some time together."

That's when I know. Is that my future, doing Dad and son things like nothing ever changed? We talk a while than I go up to the room they've booked for me. I have to report to the security services later to be interviewed. They're still not happy with my story. The problems are starting to stack up. The whole of the next day we try to act as if nothing ever happened, as if we are the same family we were back in Hong Kong. That night I make my decision. I use the phone app to book my flight. I am about to slip out of the hotel when a door opens. Anna appears in the hallway.

"How did you know?"

"I always knew you would go. I couldn't sleep. Then I heard your door open."

"I've recorded a message and sent it to your email. You won't tell them until I've gone?"

Anna shakes her head.

"In a way, I think they know too. You belong to a different world now."

I feel a buzz of electricity go through me.

"What did you say?"

"I'm not stupid, Henry. Neither is James. That time we met, he told me about some of the things Liesl showed him, some of the things she said. I remembered you playing that game. I didn't understand it. I still don't. But I knew you weren't telling the truth about the amnesia. Do what you have to do, Henry. We will always love you."

We embrace.

"Thanks. I know. I always knew."

"Even when you were calling me a pain?"

"Even then."

I walk to the lift without looking back.

An hour later I am at the airport. Three hours later I am in the air. The next day I am walking into the games shop in Wan Chai Road. Everything has changed. Everything but this shabby, little premises. I make my way upstairs. I am not surprised to see the sapphire pyramid waiting for me. I strip to my boxers and crawl inside. Minutes later I am dressing in the service area in the Presidential Palace in Thren City. I open the door and there they are, Yrin, Azari, Troya and the Arachnibrid.

Yrin grins.

"Welcome back, Henry. We will brief you while we walk to the ship."

"Where are we going?"

"To the end of the universe. This is going to make Metakal look like a walk in the park. Are you ready for it?"

I return the smile.

"Never been more ready in my life."